PAOLA CAPRIOLO was born in 1962 in Milan where she now lives. Her first book, *La grande Eulalia*, a collection of short stories, won the 1988 Giuseppe Berto Prize. *Il nocciero*, a novel, won the 1990 Rapallo prize and in 1991 Paola Capriolo was awarded the Förder Prize in Germany for her work. She is a translator and writes for the cultural pages of *Il Corriere Della Sera*.

'Capriolo has reached into the heart of the creaky melodrama on which Puccini based his opera and drawn out a darkly glistening fable of perverse obsession. High-handedly despatching the nobly suffering artist, Cavaradossi, to the margins of her text, she throws the timeworn plot dizzyingly out of kilter. The focus is now thrown entirely on to Scarpia, the merciless yet strangely compelling chief of police and his lethal erotic obsession with a morally ambivalent opera diva. Elegant, cunning and cruel, *Floria Tosca* will appeal to any opera lover who finds the virtuous heroes of the form crashing bores compared with their godless counterparts.' **Patrick Gale**

'The mechanics and pleasures of the meeting between sadist and masochist have rarely been so elegantly handled as in the story of *Tosca*. Now, reading between the lines of Sardou's melodrama and Puccini's opera, Paola Capriolo has given a new, nasty, elaborately mannered and highly entertaining twist to the classic tale of fatal attraction of policeman for diva. I suggest you put on the Callas recording, pour yourself a drink, turn the lights down, read, and surrender.' **Neil Bartlett**

'Capriolo's forte is the exquisite philosophical game played with corrosive scepticism.' *TLS*

FLORIA TOSCA

PAOLA CAPRIOLO

✤

translated by Liz Heron

This book was published with assistance from the
European Commission, Brussels

Library of Congress Catalog Card Number: 95–71062

A complete catalogue record for this book can be
obtained from the British Library on request

The right of Paola Capriolo to be identified as the author
of this work has been asserted by her in accordance
with the Copyright, Designs and Patents Act 1988

First published in Italian as *Vissi d'amore* in 1992 by Bompiani,
Milan

Copyright © 1992 Gruppo Editoriale Fabbri, Bompiani,
Sonzogno SpA
Translation copyright © 1997 Liz Heron

This edition first published in 1997 by
Serpent's Tail, 4 Blackstock Mews, London N4, and
180 Varick Street, 10th floor, New York, NY 10014

Typeset in 11pt Garamond by Intype London Limited
Printed in Great Britain by
Cox & Wyman Ltd, Reading, Berkshire

✤

PROLOGUE

✤

LATE THAT NIGHT the palace guards were roused by the thudding of a slammed door and the sound of hurried footsteps down the stairs. Whereupon they leapt out of bed and ran down the steps that led from their quarters to the entrance hall; here they saw a figure wrapped in a black cloak, intent upon opening the great door with much commotion and no apparent care for stealth. They shouted 'Halt', and the figure turned; it was a woman of rare beauty, her hair raven black, her face ashen; beneath the heavy cloak her dress flashed gold.

'What do you want?' she asked in a tone with which some queen of the Orient might address an importunate slave.

'Speak up, what is your business here at this hour? And where do you think you are going?'

'I think I am going wherever best it pleases me,' she retorted with a tremor in her voice which all of them put down to anger. 'I am so authorised by this safe conduct signed by Baron Scarpia.'

And she held out a paper on which the chief

3

of police declared that Floria Tosca, a singer by profession, was under his personal protection, and that by virtue of this protection she was at liberty to go wherever she wished, even beyond the borders of the country.

'Our apologies, madam,' said one of the guards in confusion, returning the safe conduct to her. 'We make so free as to wish you goodnight.'

With much show of deference they made way for her and closed the great door behind her as soon as she had passed outside. Only at dawn, when, upon entering the interrogation room, they found the body of Baron Scarpia pierced with a dagger and encircled in a macabre ring of candlesticks, did their thoughts turn again to the mysterious lady. At once the whole police force of the city set out to capture her, to make her pay for this abominable crime; it was unknown to all that she had already taken measures of her own to mete out justice on herself, but some days later her corpse, still bearing some remaining shreds of golden cloth, was given up by the river.

This double tragedy was long spoken of in the city, and they speak of it still, and perhaps it shall still be spoken of when the generation that witnessed it has long since passed away. Rumours, idle talk and legends became widespread, in which Floria Tosca now appeared as a sinister conspirator and enemy of the state, now as a heroine bent on self-sacrifice to topple tyranny and avenge an outraged liberty, while some saw Baron Scarpia as a staunch defender of established order, others seeing a hypocrite who made use of his own powers to procure bedroom conquests. To me alone is it vouchsafed to know how much both these parties were deluded. However, such a knowledge in my eyes is not a privilege, more a burden.

Having reached this point, I have little choice but to enter the stage as a character in my own narration, and while knowing full well that this might in some wise estrange a reader's sympathy, I am obliged to introduce myself as Scarpia's successor in the post of chief of police. Like it or not, this is my profession, and indeed it is to it that I owe the privilege or burden which I mentioned above, for thus it was granted to me to have access to the baron's study, to open the drawers of the desk after removing the seals placed there on the day following his death, and to consult the papers and documents left behind by him. Among the countless writings solely concerning matters of office, I found a thick notebook bound in black leather, and, turning its pages, I saw I had discovered a diary in which he had meticulously noted the final events in his unfortunate existence.

I read it one moonlit night, not moving from the desk until late, and when only blank pages remained before me I closed it with feelings of horror. No one, I thought, must ever come to know what turmoil filled the mind of my unhappy predecessor in those days of paroxysm: better to let him appear as a satyr, a hypocrite, a loathsome exploiter of others' misfortunes, rather than to show the world what devilishly twisted forms the virtues of a man of utter integrity and devotion to the Lord had assumed in him. I resolved upon the diary's destruction, to bring no offence to the departed man's memory, but also to preserve the dignity of an office which I myself filled.

A fire burned in the hearth; a single gesture would have been enough to silence that voice forever, yet I was unable to set my mind to do it. The heart of the matter, I reflected, was the truth, and for the truth a certain respect was also required.

The moon was high and wan, and perhaps, as I watched the clouds veil and uncover its disc, something of Scarpia's obsession managed to work its way into me. Of course I disapproved of his morbid theories, and yet I could not regard them as altogether alien. In them I had to recognise a measure, a glimmer of truth at least, something utterly different from what I had thought just before: even were it to be discovered that events had occurred as was commonly thought, even were it to be proved that the diary of Baron Scarpia was nothing but a tissue of lies confected in bad faith, out of madness, from the wish to procure some paradoxical self-vindication by transposing his own sin on to a higher sphere, none of this, it seemed to me, would have impinged upon that truth. Would it therefore have been permissible for me to suppress it? Or was it not rather my very duty to bring it to the notice of the public, if only as a warning to those who might fall victim to a fate such as this? Insidious, how dreadfully insidious, is the exercise of speculation enjoined to the exaltation of the senses, since vice is only in the spirit, not first in the flesh, and heresy is perhaps the only sin. Scarpia too, as I learned upon reading the diary, cherished ambitions of a pedagogical nature, and would have liked to educate the young to follow virtue's path. Now I could translate into practice this purpose of his in such a way as he had not foreseen, holding him up to all as an example not to be followed.

For some time I trifled with this idea, but already I knew that I should never carry it out. The sun, rising, would clear from my mind the unhealthy doubts inspired by the moonlight, restoring to me a clear sense of how much I owed to myself and to others, to my place in the world and to those through whose goodness I been given it. It would not indeed be me, I decided, who would stir up such a scandal, at that moment in particular, when the trust of the public was still shaken by the many mysteries surrounding the death of the cavaliere Cavaradossi, summarily shot with no trial on the very morning when the guards had found Scarpia's corpse. On the other hand, nor did I dare to cast the diary into the flames of the hearth: both choices entailed responsibilities too heavy for my shoulders, and in the end, after long reflection, there flashed through my mind a compromise solution which I am still of firm mind to adopt. I shall reopen the drawer and replace the diary inside it, together with these notes, then lock it, thus handing on the dilemma intact to my successor. Who is to know, perhaps a day will come when it will be possible to divulge the ravings of the baron Scarpia without danger; whosoever then will learn the truth about these tortuous goings-on, let them remember that this could have stayed forever hidden, had I not been assailed by these scruples, on that moonlit night.

✤

THE DIARY OF
BARON SCARPIA

✤

OF HER THERE IS no need to speak, but this cavaliere Cavaradossi seems to me now to have lost all restraint. His opinions, his suspect friendships, and now in addition this blasphemous gesture... I fear, alas, that the day is not far off on which it will be my thankless task to accompany the distinguished Cavaliere to the threshold of Paradise. In speaking of the other, the singer, there is nothing to be gained; doubtless she has nothing to do with political intrigues; yes, she is an accomplice of the Cavaliere, but in sins of a different nature.

Already the fact that a man of his rank should devote himself in all seriousness to the craft of the painter, publicly exhibiting his own works, is in itself a violation of the natural order, and therefore unseemly. Were he at least to refrain from dealing with religious subjects, but no, he has wished to install his lover in the house of the Lord, placing her upon an altar, and what is more showing an utter lack of regard for the very traditions of his art. Indeed, I wonder, wherever has anyone seen a painting in which the Holy Virgin is represented with those overweening features, those coal-black eyes worthy of Lucifer, or rather, since such a comparison would do overmuch honour to the model, some lesser fallen angel? If the intention is to be reproached upon religious and moral grounds, the result, it pains me to say, is also repugnant aesthetically, as always occurs when the image contrasts with the idea which it should offer to our senses instead of supporting it. In this the good Cavaradossi has revealed himself to be a painter of oxymorons, a creator of artistic contradictions, as if enough of these did not exist in this world of ours without the need for devising new ones.

But all this is irrelevant, for I went to that church without even knowing that the picture was already on display; I sought out Cavaradossi for other reasons, and it was seriously negligent of me to have forgotten this and to have left that place without any further thought to find him. For it is my office to prosecute the guilty with implacable zeal, and those who might be surmised to be so with a similarly implacable zeal, and likewise those who might be surmised to become so, since guilt spreads like a contagion, like a cancer, and in order to prevent its further transmission it is often necessary to isolate the area of infection with drastic measures. Nonetheless, the uncontrollable sense of outrage with which I was assailed before that desecration might well excuse my neglect of duty.

The church was dark, there was no one at prayer

in the naves or before the main altar, where the few lighted candles pierced the darkness with sombrely gleaming points of gold. Anyone else would certainly have concluded that no living soul was in that place, which would have been most likely besides, since this was a church that was little frequented. The main door was of a magnificence ill-befitting the alleyway on to which it opened, this being too narrow to admit the passing of carriages, while on every side this temple is hemmed in by the crumbling walls of houses such that as I entered I had wondered whether the eye of God might notice it, whether He himself might be ignorant of its existence or have forgotten it. It was moreover the early afternoon and long hot hours lay ahead before the celebration of the Vespers, hours in which only policemen and conspirators would venture out on the scorched cobbled streets, beneath a sky that the sun's rays corroded. But I am a hunter of men, from habit and, I dare to say, from vocation; I can discern the presence of my fellows, especially when they hide, with the same unerring sense with which a good dog scents the trail of game, and therefore I knew at once that, despite appearances, the church was not empty.

I set about scanning all the aisles, peering through the gratings of the closed chapels, scouring the pews to see whether anyone had left behind some object, a handkerchief, a fan, or perhaps a painter's brush; in other words I carried out the customary procedures to confirm what I already knew for certain within myself, that the cavaliere Cavaradossi, the famous painter and notorious miscreant, was hidden within those walls or had only just fled, startled by the sound of my footsteps. Indeed when the sinner himself has departed there still remains for some time that metaphysical odour thanks to which I have already consigned so many sinners' bodies to justice and entrusted their souls to divine mercy, and what I now perceived was without a doubt the odour of Cavaradossi, or of something which belonged to him so intimately as to be by now permeated with it. Of this, in fact, I had confirmation almost at once.

I had found open the gate of one of the first chapels on the left nave, and, taking care lest it creak, I had entered; from there, through the gratings which separated one from the other, I had been able, unobserved, to observe the whole line of chapels. I was untroubled by the darkness, for my nature, though it has a side akin to the bloodhound, has another which resembles the more cunning ways of the cat, and of felines in general, and so that I might better carry out my earthly task, God has given me eyes able to make out shapes and movements even in the dark. But scarcely had I crossed the gate when I realised that I would have no need of recourse to such faculties: in the adjacent chapel a long row of candles was lit before the altar, and kneeling at the first pew, her face almost touched by the flames, was she, Floria Tosca, the singer. Perhaps Cavaradossi had left her behind instead of the brush, a handkerchief or some other object of his. I deemed it a fortunate chance, since a trace endowed with speech is without doubt more useful, if properly made use of, than a mute trace.

I had seen her before, in the street or at receptions

in certain patrician houses where she had made use of her vocal talents to insinuate herself, but I had never spoken to her, nor had I joined the crowd of those infatuated persons who rushed to the theatre to applaud her every time her name should appear on some playbill. Now however I would have to approach her and question her. Duty imposed it. Besides, the thought of this did not worry me, certain as I was that I would know how to resist the allure of that voice, triumph over it, bend it with the subtle art of persuasion to reveal to me all that it would wish to keep silent.

Even less was I troubled by the seductions of her appearance; these had always left me indifferent, and against the prevailing opinion, I instead take it upon myself even to deny their existence. Female beauty is harmony, a limpid mirror of the harmony of creation, but Tosca is all dissonance and unresolved contrasts. An impression due above all to that mass of black hair which crowns the palest of faces, a black so deep as to provoke a certain disgust in those who look upon it, an impression augmented by those ardent eyes of hers, as if she were at all times intent on singing duets of unbridled passion with some invisible companion. All of this appears designed to be in keeping with the tastes of our times: the people have a surfeit, it would seem, of the simple grace of virtue, which is scorned as something cloying, and instead seek out morbid attractions which reflect vice, excess and an inner deformity.

And yet at that moment, seeing her rapt in prayer, I could not stop myself from contemplating Tosca with different eyes. I had approached the grating on tiptoe, lest she notice my presence. Her form melted into the darkness, from which there issued only her joined hands and her face, with the reddish light of the candles gathered upon it, and it seemed to me to find there an expression which was singularly sweet, of serene beatitude.

I had heard talk that Tosca, for all the dissolute life she led, was a pious person who frequented churches with scrupulous regularity, yet in this conduct I had always suspected a pose, an affectation. By parading, between her acts of wantonness, contrition and fear of God, perhaps she deceived herself that she could swindle the Father Eternal, or perhaps she hoped only to increase her own charms by adding a new contrast to those that were already in her nature, to pursue by artificial means the enterprise embarked upon, doubtless distractedly, by her Creator, when He gave her eyes and hair so black and skin so white. Now instead I recognised in her the spark of a real faith and it came to my mind that her piety would procure for her forgiveness for many sins, so that one day, should He whose irrevocable sentence I await judge me worthy to contemplate His glory, I would find Floria Tosca, the singer, the lover of Cavaradossi, seated, by virtue of that pure spark, in the circle of the blessed souls.

I started towards her, resolved now to speak to her in tones quite different from those I had at first meant to employ: not as the judge who addresses the reprobate to wrench from him the confession of his misdeeds, but as the doctor addresses the patient, or the brother a sister who has fallen but who remains very dear. I made up my mind not to disturb her at prayer, and to wait respectfully in the nave until she herself should come towards me.

When I stood before the chapel where I had noticed her I stopped to observe its interior. Tosca was still on her knees, engaged in reciting a quiet litany. Beneath her veil I glimpsed the outline of her shoulders and her head held high, lifted towards the altar where the reflection of the candles shone upon the cornice of a painting. She raised her voice a little at one point in the prayer, stressing the words with clarity: '*Benedicta tu in mulieribus*', she said in that voice of hers with its warm, deep timbre, which for the first time succeeded in moving me. Obviously the unfortunate woman's prayer was addressed to the image of the Holy Virgin, and indeed, as I looked with greater attention, I discerned on the canvas above the altar a female figure dressed in a tunic of gold. I took a few steps forward the better to see it.

Perhaps Tosca heard me; I had the impression that she moved, but I took no notice, nor was I troubled by the thought of having broken into her prayer. I stared at the picture with incredulity and anger, with my blood running cold, wondering how Cavaradossi could have dared to give to the Mother of God the features of the woman who was his companion in illicit pleasures, and how that same woman could have dared to kneel at prayer in front of her own portrait. Because the image up above the altar, taking in vain the holy name of Maria, was in truth the image of Tosca reproduced with absolute fidelity, down to the long flowing raven-black hair, whose tresses fell uncovered by any veil around the pale white face and on the cloak of an indigo hue so dark as to appear black. In the ecstatic expression with which the painter had given life to the features of the Virgin I recognised the self-same one which I had perceived just before when spying upon Tosca, but only now did that ecstasy reveal its nature as in no way virginal. Each detail displayed exultation, voluptuousness and infinite self-regard: the fleshy lips, painted with exaggerated realism, seemed about to open in an ambiguous smile, and the eyelids were half closed over the glittering eyes. It was not hard for me to guess in what circumstances, in the course of what licentious congress the painter had seen that expression on the face of his model.

'*Benedicta tu in mulieribus*', I whispered indignantly, and Tosca must have heard me, for she hurriedly made the sign of the cross and rose. Inexplicably I was unable to bear the thought of finding myself face to face with her and, quite forgetting the reason that had brought me to that church, I moved towards the entrance, almost running. When I reached the great wooden doors I stopped; all at once I saw I could not leave without meeting Tosca, without holding her eyes for a moment at least. My self-respect, my dignity as a man, made it imperative to remain and wait for her. I positioned myself next to the holy water font, thus compelling her to pass by me on her way out.

I kept my eyes on her as she came down the aisle. Just then I saw her falter, and I realised that she had recognised me; she too apparently possessed eyes able to make out shapes in the dark, like cats, like nocturnal animals. From the dark dress she wore and from the raven-black abundance of hair to be discerned beneath her veil, she seemed even darker than the darkness of the church, as if it were she who irradiated that shadow in the same way as the stars irradiate light.

Deliberately, I left the entrance door ajar to let in a ray of sunlight that would illuminate the face of Tosca. I saw her lift an arm to shade her eyes; then she continued walking, but more slowly. Perhaps she was frightened, yet her bearing remained proud, almost disdainful. She would not turn back, I was sure of it, she would not look for some side door, she would come right up to me, overcoming apprehension, out of some feeling not dissimilar from the one that kept me there. Determination endowed her demeanour with an aura of majesty, and as I watched her I found it hard to see in that haughty creature the woman who was ready to surrender so easily to Cavaradossi and his predecessors. I should rather have imagined her as practising that brand of virtue or rather that simulacrum of it whose innermost spring is a boundless arrogance.

When she arrived beside me Tosca pretended not to see me and made as if to proceed, but I was quick to block her way. I dipped my hand in the holy water font and held it out to her in an act of offering, so that she was compelled to reach hers towards me to accept the holy water. She did not withdraw her palm from mine immediately, she did not lower her eyes as I stared at her; she remained motionless, yet I felt a slight tremor in her hand. At last she removed it abruptly, and without crossing herself left the church.

MY OFFICE, WHOSE vital importance for collective wellbeing is so obvious as to require no explanation, is continually impeded by a disproportionate number of petitions which day after day pile up upon my desk. Often have I thought of entrusting this weighty correspondence to a secretary, but I have never been able to make up my mind to take such a step; a secretary would not know how to bring comfort to those afflicted souls as I do, showing them logically that affliction such as theirs is but the fruit of a shortsighted gaze, obfuscated by an undue overestimation of their own personal case, and incapable of perceiving its irrelevance in relation to the higher economy of the whole.

Is it not perhaps arrogance, natural as it may be and in some sense excusable, to claim that the universal order of things should undergo an exception for their sake or that of their dear ones, and that it should even be suspended should it threaten affections, liberty or life? Does he not perhaps commit the sin of pride whosoever, before this universal order, instead of bowing down in silence or, if need be, making willing self-sacrifice, dares to raise his voice and pronounce the word 'I'? As if this 'I' were not, in each and every case, the most negligible entity in the world.

Thus A cannot be condemned, because 'I' would die of unhappiness and it falls to me patiently to remind the illustrious Signor 'I' that there would be nothing extraordinary in this, that sooner or later, alas, such a fate would in any case be his; B has to be spared from torture in order not to disturb 'I' and his delicate sensitivity, and poor Scarpia, instead of attending to his own duties in peace, must dedicate a whole hour to teaching the petitioner some resignation and Christian humility, to showing him, more often than not to no purpose, what a sublime thought is enclosed in the words 'Let Thy will be done'. Even Christ, in the garden at Gethsemane, spoke those words: 'Let Thy will, not mine, be done'; and Christ, it must be allowed, even only regarded in his human nature, was an 'I' much more relevant and worthy, if anyone ever was, of seeing the chalice of suffering taken from his lips.

This work of consolation to which I dedicate myself is particularly arduous with women, whose intellect, weaker than that of man, lacks the means to raise itself through reflection above the singularity of its own fate. Today for example, entering my study a little before dawn, I found on the desk the harrowing pleas of a mother appealing to me for mercy. And the appeal, as I hastened to assure her, will not go unheard. Indeed, I answered her, by sending your son to his death I act from no whim, but, through official channels, I obey the will of God. Or perhaps you suppose that it gives me some pleasure to send your unfortunate son to his death? (It is a common enough mistake, there are many who take my zeal for cruelty.) Assuming that, as I hope, you do not suppose this, I can conduct my argument to its conclusion:

First premiss: in having your son condemned I obey the will of God.

Second premiss: God is supreme mercy (on this at least you will agree: should this not be the case, I keenly urge you to speak of it with your confessor).

Conclusion: by condemning your son to death I act in keeping with divine mercy, and as a consequence my action is itself merciful, Q.E.D. If instead I were to spare him I should be disobeying the Lord, and consequently, as can be deduced from the second premiss, I should violate the laws of mercy. God preserve me from committing such a sin, and God preserve you from wishing me to commit it! Combat human weaknesses, Signora, and lift up your eyes to the eternal recompense which will undoubtedly be accorded you if you can bend your will and submit to this trial. In the meantime be so good as to accept the most sincere regards of Your . . .

By good fortune nature has given to women, perhaps to compensate them for their vulnerability, a defence with which we men are equipped in somewhat lesser measure. I refer to that peculiar voluptuous pleasure which, as I have often observed, they can derive from suffering, and which the better disposes them to receive its redemptive virtue. Their desire for submission, while making them more inclined to sin, on the other hand, so long as properly guided, leads them to face the torments of atonement and the mortification of the body and the spirit, with an almost joyful patience, as if not merely confining themselves to acceptance of the means for the sake of the end, but going so far as to love the means in itself, relishing tortures and finding happiness in penance. Without doubt purgatory is seething with these afflicted and pleasure-loving souls who display no haste to be admitted to Heaven, and perhaps hell too is seething with them. It is strange how from a single root there can germinate the most subtly abject vice and the most sublime virtue. As for myself, I am very far from such extremes; I can exercise humility and contrition, it is true, and can induce my neighbour to exercise them also, yet I practise both of these things without the passion of the saint or the sinner, out of pure and sober observance of my duty.

I replace the poor mother's petition in the drawer. The date of execution will need to be brought forward so as to relieve her of this painful uncertainty, and so that she will have no time to write to me again.

The sun must already be high, and the multitude of Is must have been busily at work for some hours now. They take up their pens to express to Baron Scarpia their little thoughts on what is just or unjust, to tell him their little troubles; they protest to him against the universal order, and then reward his kind words by calumny and accusations of his inhumanity and cruelty. But here, thanks be to God, everything of this reaches me only indirectly, even the light is hard put to enter through the velvet drapes which screen the windows. I prefer to work by candlelight even in the middle of the day, but feeling alone, far from the world and its chattering.

My men are allowed to enter this room only when I am not here, in order to leave on the desk, besides letters, brief messages in which they request instructions or inform me about a task carried out. I write out my orders and before retiring I leave them on the desk, so that they will find them there on the following day. Not even at times of greatest import have I permitted anyone to infringe this rule, convinced as I am that a rigid and unalterable discipline is a necessary condition for the success of any enterprise whatsoever. Likewise I go upstairs always at fixed times, thrice a day, at intervals of eight hours, and remain there for forty minutes. No longer is ever needed.

I leaf through last night's reports, without finding anything especially relevant: Angelotti, as was to be expected, has decided to sign the confession; the execution of Count Palmieri has been fixed for Thursday; *Maria Triumphant*, oil on canvas by Mario Cavaradossi, representing the Madonna in the act of crushing the serpent, exhibited in the chapel of the Attavanti family at the church of San ... Maria Triumphant, no less! It would have been more fitting for him to have sought inspiration in the holy sorrows: thus he would have made some display, if not of talent, of prophetic virtue.

Some strange indolence continues to draw me away from my papers and drive me back to the pages of this journal; even during the interrogation this morning I was distracted, almost negligent of what was happening around me, so much was I compelled by my desire to return here and resume writing. And yet I have nothing to say, or at least, nothing especially relevant.

This room is over-sumptuous; I had already observed this on other occasions, but today its splendour disturbs me and oppresses my senses. Too much gold on the pillars and the door jambs, on the heavy frames of the pictures, and above all too many drapes of red velvet. It is as if I am imprisoned between the curtains of a theatre stage. I have not altered my opinion, I am still convinced that it is well to satisfy, where possible, the whims wherein our earthly wretchedness contains us, so as to avoid the refusal by reality that might drive them to find refuge in the imagination and there be magnified. I acted therefore with utmost prudence when, in furnishing the study, I chose to gratify my desire for luxury instead of suppressing it; an extremely innocent desire, if innocent desires do ever exist. But today that vision of the theatre returns repeatedly before my eyes and I cannot put it from me, surely because of all these scarlet coloured drapes.

It is disconcerting, the power that objects have to weave connections one between the other so as to form a net in which one might easily be snared. Yet, patently, objects would not have such power did our imagination not invest it in them, and therefore, by the by, we cannot compare the theatre to the brothel, as is the wont of certain dull-minded bigots to do. The comparison does not hold good, because the theatre is infinitely more insidious. For indeed, where the harlot undertakes to quench those lusts which are alas the legacy of every man since the day that Adam fell, the actress or worse still, the singer, inflames new ones, deceiving the eye with seductions of artifice, with revealing and opulent costumes, deceiving the ear with ardent words and caressing melodies, and above all joining forces with imagination, that cursed faculty, that hotbed of corruption buried in each one of us, reawakening it, exciting it, so that when the curtain falls and we leave our theatre seats we find ourselves in a state of mind much more harmful to eternal salvation than when we had arrived. This at least is what I remember; the truth is that, having learned enough from my first experience, I have not set foot in the theatre for some thirty years.

Therefore, to conclude: frequent, if you truly must, the harlot, and go to her without care, as if you were taking the cure of the waters, but avoid the actress and even more the singer. (Perhaps some day, when I have retired to the country, I shall develop this idea in a brief treatise for the edification of the young, so as to be useful to others in old age as I am now, in the bloom of maturity.) If you cannot but do so, visit the brothel, but stay away from the theatre, for often the image of a thing does greater harm than the thing itself, transplanting itself into the soul with greater facility and taking firm root there. The existence of the image, contrary to that of the thing, has no limit in either time or space, it multiplies and perpetuates itself to infinity, and if, let us suppose, it happens that you see a woman and also her portrait or reflection in a mirror, that portrait or reflection will live on in you much longer than the woman herself, and not even were she to cease to be would it altogether disappear. I have chosen this example, but I could have cited others quite at random; for when one reasons on matters of common interest that are bound up with the universal order, examples in themselves have not the least importance.

I have never been fond of taking walks, seldom do I leave the building unless obliged by some errand. The most delicate investigations of course must be carried out by myself in person, and I do not deny that to put my capacity thus to the test is for me a source of great pleasure; but once a matter is set in motion I prefer to remain in my study, with the door firmly shut, and from here, detached and invisible, like Providence, to decide the fate of others.

Of course this is a matter of taste: my distinguished predecessors experienced an inordinate pleasure in carrying out the capture in person; this is a somewhat puerile inclination, since to feel oneself the author of an act one need not play a part in its material execution; it only has to be acknowledged as a direct consequence of one's own will. Thus I do not stir, I am not vexed or bothered; here, armed with patience, I await the faultless fulfilment of my commands.

When all is said and done, Scarpia's life, to his

deep satisfaction, keeps a somewhat monotonous course, also thanks to the guilty who are all alike; my usual comings and goings consist merely of climbing and descending the flight of stairs that lead from the study to the floor above, where I conduct interrogations with a procedure which never varies. It is therefore still unclear to me why, at dusk, I suddenly decided to go out, without this decision in any way being justified by the investigations in which I am engaged. Perhaps I could no longer bear to see the gold, or the red of the drapes, and I left the building to seek solace in the poverty of the alleyways. I did not find it. In these times no longer even does poverty know the grace of simplicity, but it disports itself in twisted arabesques, in immoderate flourishes, and from the hovels that line the alleyways, former patrician dwellings now invaded by the rabble, there once more, aggressively, in a form corrupt and cankered, was the splendour from which I had wished to flee. In the courtyards, an untidy flora of palm trees and climbing plants seemed to draw from the heavy summer air an unwholesome nourishment, everything extravagantly overgrown, suffocated by its own luxuriance, and not only the plants, but the dilapidated walls of the houses, on whose cracked marble stairs ragged children played, and the brightly coloured linen hung out to dry on the balconies, shamelessly displaying stains and patches, all of this expressed a fervour of decay, a funereal vitality.

The layers of ruins that have slowly settled one upon the other, the decay of centuries and millennia, make of these places a ground so fertile that any seed whatsoever could develop and prosper in it, and each thing grows there serenely together with its opposite, reconciled with it through the infinite tolerance of decomposition. Thus I was unamazed to see, just opposite a house on whose threshold a fat woman sat in her shift with her feet plunged in a basin, the façade of a church, looking straight at me, as if to remind me of the existence of a more worthy world, nor was I amazed as I recognised the church and thought again of the painting which I knew was kept within it; only now that temple no longer seemed to me in contrast with the corruption with which it was surrounded, but to belong to it closely. I looked again at the woman with her feet in the basin; sooner or later, I told myself, some shoddy painter would choose her as a model for a portrait of Saint Anne or Saint Genevieve. Did not some sage pagan write that had oxen and horses hands to build the images of their gods, they would represent them in the likeness of oxen or horses? And those urchins wallowing in the mire, apprentice pickpockets, future pimps or bandits, were so many Infant Jesuses, to put upon altars.

Of course, the singer is altogether different: she does not wallow in the mire, but in the gold and gems given to her by her lovers, and she would never show herself half-undressed in a doorway, with her feet in a basin, preferring to sell dear the privilege of regarding her nakedness. And yet she too, only now did I remember, lives in that alleyway, a few yards from the church. A convenient enough location, so near to the place where the Cavaliere is wont to lavish time and talent for the greater glory of the faith. I wondered whether Tosca had chosen that lodging because Cavaradossi worked in the church, or whether instead it was Cavaradossi who had accepted that commission because from the church he could make frequent visits to Tosca's apartments.

I turned my back on the profane temple, while in the sky the light of day was dimming. The woman took her feet out of the water, got up, picked up the chair in one hand and the basin in the other, went back inside the house and closed the door behind her. Even the urchins had disappeared. Now no one passed through the alleyway, but from the open windows, besides the odour of frying, there came a clamour of equal unpleasantness. Undoubtedly these were families assembled around the table to consume their meagre supper, and yet everyone shouted, as if to make themselves heard from the top of a bell tower by some neighbour left down in the churchyard.

It was time too for me to make my way home. I walked a short way down the alleyway and it happened that I passed before the building where Tosca lives. Pale curtains, of muslin, screened the windows of her lodging. Just at that moment, a servant issued from the doorway carrying a letter. I blocked his path.

'Where are you going, my good man?'

'Why?' he answered in insolent tones. 'Can it be that I have to give an account of where I go to you?'

All have to give account to me, should I wish it; but I deemed it opportune not to frighten the servant by revealing my identity, and so I said nothing;

instead, as blandishment, I reached out and handed him a silver coin.

'However,' he added, after pocketing it, 'if you really must know, I am going to deliver this letter.'

'From whom?'

'My mistress.'

'And who might your mistress be?'

I was compelled to dole out another coin to induce him to utter the venerated name of Floria Tosca.

'To whom must you deliver the letter?'

'To a gentleman,' he answered laconically.

'Of this, be assured, I have no doubt. But perhaps with a little goodwill you could tell me more.'

'It falls to you, sir, to give proof of goodwill.'

'And have I not given you enough?'

'It depends, sir, what it is you wish to know. In exchange for the goodwill shown up until now, I can only tell you that it concerns a person of rank, a nobleman.'

Cavaradossi, doubtless. My mind made up, I took a gold coin from my purse. 'Would this, in your opinion, be sufficient reason to entrust me with the letter and allow me to be the one to deliver it to that nobleman?'

He looked at the coin with an air of condescension, without deigning to take it. I added two more, although his greed exasperated me, and in the end he consented to the exchange.

He made off in great haste while, in the half light, I strove to decipher the name written on the envelope. At last I could read: 'To The Most Illustrious Baron Scarpia'. So I had squandered my skills of persuasion and paid three gold coins and two silver ones in order to intercept a letter addressed to me. Of all my undertakings this one alone would I have hidden from those who come after me.

I opened the envelope. In the letter Tosca declared that she needed to speak to me urgently. And begged me to join her in her dressing-room after the performance. She had included an invitation to the theatre.

I screwed up the letter, the envelope and the invitation and threw them onto the cobblestones, new filth going the same way as the old. I in the theatre, what an idea. And in obedience to the promptings of madame the singer. At times I am fond of visiting such personages, but when these are unexpected visits and altogether unwished for. Like that evening when, on the trail of a famous violinist suspected of subversive opinions, I went to the reception of an ambassador where he had been invited to perform. I stopped on the threshold of the room and as soon as he saw me he stopped, his bow raised, frozen in movement. He was reputed to be the idol of the ladies, yet in that moment there was not a single one of them who accorded him a look; they were all staring at me, Scarpia the cruel, Scarpia the inhuman, and likewise did their gentlemen. It is an episode to which my thoughts always return with pleasure.

I looked up at Tosca's windows. In one of the rooms a light was lit, casting a female shadow on the curtains. A maid, I surmised, but on closer observation I thought to discern, behind the very clearly defined profile, a mass of hair that was long and loose; since it is not customary for maids to go about dishevelled in the houses where they serve I recognised in that black silhouette the lady of the house in person, Tosca Triumphant.

I saw her sit down at a small table and take up an object; then she raised an arm to the top of her head and slowly drew it back down, following the outline of her hair, raising and lowering it once more, and raising it again, and so on, always with that slow, almost hieratic gesture. In front of her there must have been a mirror in which she was admiring herself, congratulating herself on her own beauty, knowing herself because of it, to be blessed among women.

I could not take my eyes off that window. When Tosca lifted the comb, the broad sleeve of her gown fell away, leaving bare to the elbow an arm that was slender and well shaped, narrow at the wrist. I had to admit that when the Creator was sculpting her body, he had worked with a fine chisel; the soul instead was marble, as yet unhewn, or more likely had been refined by quite a different hand and led by it to a certain negative perfection. From her posture, from the soft movement with which she let the comb run through her hair, there was apparent a coquetry so deep-rooted as to be by now transformed into an instinct, for Tosca was alone for sure, and nor could she know that I was watching from the street. She was staging that seductive ritual for her own sake alone.

I was deluded. After some moments, another figure, this time a male one, appeared within the space of the light and went to sit beside her. Indeed he sat so close to her that the two shadows almost merged into one, a double-headed monster from which I averted my eyes in disgust.

One half of the monster was doubtless Cavara-dossi, a man as good as dead, who, unaware of the danger, continued to practise his chosen amuse-ments. Evidently, even though he makes public show of being a learned man profoundly acquainted with the most modern philosophies, the Cavaliere is unaware of having become, precisely by virtue of so public a show, a suspect person, and is unaware of how short is the step from the condition of suspect to that of self-confessed criminal. A step which we shall find the means to quicken.

For some time I had been profoundly convinced of his guilt, alas however my profound conviction does not constitute a proof, and in reviewing the facts I had to conclude yet again that I lacked suf-ficient evidence to incriminate the Cavaliere. It was therefore necessary to find others, but by what means? By waiting to surprise him committing some grave imprudence? Before then, however, months, perhaps years could have passed, during which he could continue to plot against the universal order with impunity, to lead his libertine existence and visit Tosca's house each evening. So was there no shortcut? Was there no one who knew more about him than I knew and who perhaps, suitably questioned. . . .?

Once again I looked up at the window. The light had been extinguished, the two black silhouettes had disappeared, swallowed up in the blackness of the room. The alleyway too appeared in darkness, but on inspecting the ground I managed to discern the invitation which Tosca had sent me, and I bent to pick it up. I also picked up the letter; I smoothed it with my hands, folded it again and hid it beneath my waistcoat.

So, after so long, the inexorability of fate and the inevitability of duty would take me back to a place where I would never have wished to return. The thought produced in me a turmoil which, I must confess, was also not altogether disagreeable. Certainly, for reasons upon which I have already dwelt sufficiently, I should be much calmer were Tosca to have given me an appointment in a brothel, but providence cannot always take account of our tastes. Besides, it was precisely the extreme perniciousness of the place I would have to go to that excited in me a taste for adventure, a desire to put myself to the test, to fight, to triumph. Scarpia Triumphant: a subject to bring before the attention of the eminent Cavaradossi.

From the profuse vegetation of the courtyards there now came a sharp and cloying perfume, which went to my head and yet invigorated me. My blood seemed to run faster, while this superabundant vitality did not achieve translation into a greater energy of the limbs, which by contrast remained as if dulled, but was entirely absorbed by the activity of the senses which had been suddenly opened to take in everything around them. It seemed to me almost, and this sensation was not altogether disagreeable, that I had been transformed from an individual capable of action and able to assure his own solidity, into a mass of soft melted wax on which anything could freely stamp its impress. The

smells, sights and sounds of the alleyway flowed
into me, crowding together, piling one on to the
other, and I no longer perceived the wretchedness
of details, but only the intensity of the whole; it
urged inertia and forgetfulness upon me, akin to the
eternal immobility of a stone which lets time run
over it.

On a balcony two emaciated children are playing
with an equally emaciated dog; at a window a
woman lifts her arm, perhaps she too to comb her
hair; on a wall, a cascade of white bellflowers already
yellowed at the edges waits for putrefaction to come
and free it from the empty labour of survival, and
each thing around here seems to await the same
release, to draw a hidden splendour from the same
intimations.

My eyes turned upwards again. Over the half
mourning of the earth there stretched the deep
mourning of the sky, nothingness over the hope of
nothingness. Just then the moon's disc, a darkish
red, rose from behind a hill; it rose slowly, without
any radiance of light. Then I thought of Tosca, of
Cavaradossi, of Scarpia; I brought them to mind
as remote figures, as characters in some imaginary
happening represented on the stage of a theatre, in
a blaze of false lights surrounded by the truth of
darkness, and I thought that to bring them thus to
mind was not altogether disagreeable.

I ARRANGED IT so that I reached the theatre during the third act of the opera. I was unconcerned to witness the conclusion, which I foresaw as bloody, of the musical drama *The Triumph of Virtue*, but I had been seized by a certain curiosity to see Floria Tosca on stage, and hear her in one of her famous roles. More out of habit than from necessity I had by then apprised myself in detail of all who played a part in the performance, even down to the stage attendants. A formality of the kind could not besides be overlooked, for my visit to the theatre was no foolish urge for entertainment, but an observance of the duties bound by my profession.

Of the singers, musicians and stage attendants I learned nothing of any interest. The composer it seemed was a cousin of some pupil of a famous German musician who writes opera in the Italian style in France. As for the two librettists, for want of distinguished family connections, their claim to glory derived from their prodigiously prolific talent; together they have so far created fifty libretti for *opera seria* and twenty-two for *opera buffa*, some, it is said, in less than three hours. This aside, I do not find them to be due any other kind of recognition.

From the silent entrance hall, so heavily stuccoed and gilded as to eclipse my dreams of opulence, an usher led me to a curving corridor where the notes of the orchestra could scarcely be heard, muffled as they were by the thickly padded hangings which curtained the doors, and then into the box to which Floria Tosca had had the goodness to invite me.

Now the music was really deafening. Directly beneath me I could see the gleam of the brass instruments and the warmer more subdued sparkle of the strings, I could see the scored parts spread open on the music stands and the impassioned movement of arms as if in an access of collective madness. The notes came swirling in rapid succession, almost dissonant; against the dark, insistent murmur of the double basses there rose the screech of violins, rhythmic yet bringing a sense of disorder and violent commotion, like the throbbing of a giant heart in the grip of some appalling dread.

While the heartbeats quickened I set myself to watch the stage, which in somewhat rudimentary fashion, was intended to depict a garden: papier-mâché trees and bushes scattered here and there, in one corner some form of temple or pavilion in Corinthian style, and a great dark backdrop to simulate the night sky, in which a white circle, through which rays of lamplight weakly shone, did duty for the moon. She was standing in the middle of the stage, the features of her face made hazy by dimness through which her eyes alone were to be discerned. In recompense her figure, dressed scantily in a tunic of gold, stood out in a manner which was even exaggerated. Her arms and shoulders were naked; her bosom, of which much was bare, drew the yellowish reflections of the tunic and appeared to be strewn with a fine sparkling dust.

For a long time, while the orchestra eddied in dramatic crescendo, Tosca held the total stillness of some idol who stood there to be worshipped. Then the music grew softer, and she brought her hands to her breast, to claim that whole tumult of notes for herself, for some secret personal torment.

The nature of this torment was revealed to me and to the rest of the audience in the stilted verses of a recitative which Tosca intoned with her face turned three-quarters away from those watching, in an attitude of modest withdrawal, as if the enormity of what she had to say would not allow her to meet the eyes of spectators. Her voice too was meek and low.

'What horror unconfined, oh mighty gods,
your will assigns to my unhappy self! Amid love's
zephyrs soft
I see I can no longer tarry:
in wretchedness, hell's cruel torments
I'll defy, to bring death's hand
and spare my life from dire
fate decreed by wicked heart of man.'

What a strange theology, I thought was that of the two librettists: a world without a god and yet wherein exist the pains of hell, where beneath a

heaven that is empty, or filled with guilesome simul-
acra, souls in trembling await eternal damnation.
Even though, quite patently, the idea of God is con-
tained within that of eternal damnation, and the
sinner who sees himself as such perhaps already is
the most incontrovertible proof of His existence.

A peremptory gesture cut short my reflections:
with a semblance of challenge Tosca stretched out
her arms to the audience, the palms of her hands
held open. Now she seemed no longer to feel shame,
but rather asked for complicity, and her song caress-
ingly mingled with that of the first violin:

'Must these gentle hands,
pure and unsullied
as they are, shed blood?
Oh woeful hands of mine!'

Rather than caressing, it was alluring, even self-
satisfied, and the soft deep timbre seemed to imply
less some impending threat than an obscure promise
of beatitude. I was disturbed by it, and yet I deemed
that tone to be natural, almost inevitable for those
words. Moreover I could not dispel the strange
impression that as Tosca sang she kept her eyes all
the while upon the box where I was seated.

'Must these dainty hands be raised
in vengeance?
To plunge into the villain's blood?
Oh gods, come to my aid!'

What ferocity this conjures, yet with it what
sweetness! Lovely and majestic in the vigour of
her murderous purpose, unbeknown to herself

Cavaradossi's lover embodied the most sublime ideal of justice, and if in my mind I mocked the ill-made verses, my heart was more and more won over to the heroine's cause. The plot, I thought, was not without nobility, and it is doubtless worthy to remind this throng of the depraved that virtue is ever fated to triumph over vice. I felt a genuine satisfaction in picturing the little gentle hands raised in vengeance, and armed, one imagines, with a dagger to wreak havoc on that 'villain' whose misdeed I did not even know; an office not dissimilar from the one which I myself perform each day, although with hands less graceful and without any musical accompaniment.

Several times Tosca repeated the two couplets of the aria, enriching them with ever new variations and embellishments and showing a particular fondness for the verse: 'To plunge into the villain's blood'. In the final invocation to the pagan gods she made her voice quiver, as if overwrought with turbulent emotion, something which provoked boundless enthusiasm in the audience. In the whole theatre, I alone refrained from applauding.

But events followed swiftly; the villain, accompanied by solemn music, made his entrance onstage in the person of a fat old castrato with the voice of a contralto, whose looks remained kindly however much he tried to give his face an attitude of fierceness.

'I come, my lady, to our tryst:
my passion there will be appeased',

he sang with threatening lustfulness, meanwhile

advancing towards her, his cloak flapping at the edges like the wings of some nocturnal bird.

Tosca hesitated; for a moment it seemed she had forgotten her lines. At last she answered, but her voice was faint and strangely cracked.

'To the knave's desire
my virtue shall not yield,'

she confided in the audience, and then, turning to the contralto:

'My word I always honour:
the gods so will it.'

Now beside his companion, the seducer put an arm around her naked shoulders and drew her to him. She shuddered ostentatiously, which did not prevent the orchestra from commenting on this turn of events by launching into a swelling melody.

'To the night's dark mantle,
to the moon's bright glow,
I sing out loud and joyful
as drunk on love I go'

the contralto repeated in ecstasy, and over his voice there came Tosca's disconsolate one:

'To the night's dark mantle,
to the moon's bright glow,
loud I raise lamentings doleful
suffering torment in my heart.'

And they went on to embroider on these words for a time, entwining their voices in an ever more inextricable tangle. Tosca's mane of black hair rested not only on her own shoulders but on one of the contralto's, as if she wanted in some way to bind him to herself, even while continuing to affirm feelings and intentions to the contrary. A goddess of justice with vengeance in her hands should in no circumstances recline her head on the shoulder of the evildoer and abandon herself to his embrace, languidly, forgetting all her punitive intent, and she should not express 'the torment in her heart' in such inexplicably voluptuous accents. When are we to have the stabbing? I asked myself with a degree of impatience.

At last Tosca freed herself from his embrace and pointed to the Corinthian-style temple:

> 'Before you lead me there
> (oh gods!) into the hidden temple,
> for my beloved husband,
> sire, clemency decree.'

A reasonable request from her point of view, but rather less so from that of the seducer, who would only have been sure of achieving his own ends by following the inverse procedure: *first* the tender ceremony in the little temple, *then* the signing of the pardon. I expected therefore that he would counter with a firm refusal, but instead he answered candidly:

> 'Dearest one, it takes no time at all,
> here is the paper you desire!
> Oh happy night,
> night of voluptuous pleasures!'

In the face of that disarming trust, which was so ill met, I firmly changed sides: my sympathies were now with the villain, the victim of a vulgar ruse, while I was ever more disgusted with the falseness and gratuitous flirtatiousness of she who should have made herself the instrument of divine chastisement. When ever did I, in the course of interrogation, languidly lay my head upon the shoulder of the one being questioned? And was it really necessary to point to 'the hidden temple' with that inviting and suggestive gesture, more befitting some practised harlot than a tragic heroine. Is it fated that every time I let myself be drawn to admiration of this woman it is only to discover her irredeemable abjection.

The castrato took Tosca by the hand, making ready to lead her towards the little temple; a not unfair claim, given that she by then had made haste to take possession of the pardon and hide it in her breast. But here she is again, putting on that air of outrage, here she is resisting and protesting, as the opening melody was heard once more with its breathless throbbing.

'My darling, what now troubles you?'

the seducer politely enquires.

'Take pity on my suffering!'

At this point the contralto too yields to a just indignation:

'Pity? That can never be!'
'Alas, hear now my plea!'

At first she threatens with a look, then her words beseech, and now she abandons herself to a long and clamorous invective to which the seducer lends an over-patient ear:

'Vile wretch, to what avail
do you enjoy this suffering of mine?
The heavens' countenance turns pale
on seeing your dreadful crime!'

It seemed to me that when she repeated the couplet for the third time Tosca replaced the words 'on seeing your dreadful crime' with 'on seeing your delightful crime', and I wondered whether this was the singer's own slip of the tongue or some variation devised by the two indefatigable librettists. A delightful crime: this was precisely my own state of mind as I watched Tosca turn with ample, sorrowful gestures now towards her companion, now towards the audience, now towards the painted night sky, and it was criminal delight that she herself seemed to be feeling, whether at the idea of yielding to the ardour of the wrongdoer or at the thought of taking up a bloody vendetta against him. My mind, dizzied by Tosca's high notes, was at a loss to make out any clear distinction between the two solutions.

But the aria was now over, and the contralto responded in kind with the execution of vocal acrobatics between notes at opposite ends of the scale:

'End your entreaties, madam, they are vain:
I fear not the pangs of remorse.
It is love's great and sweetest recourse
fearless to stand defying hell.'

And Tosca, ready, with the same melody:

'I end, vile wretch, my vain entreaties,
I set my mind upon a violent course.
Fear of retribution loses all its force:
my honour I'll avenge!'

With this song on her lips she drew the longed-for dagger from a hidden fold in her tunic and with it pierced the evildoer, to the accompaniment of a fortissimo which gradually faded away as the unhappy man sank to the ground. Then the latter sat up and murmured superfluously:

'I die, ill-fated!'

Icy, her head held high, Tosca retorted:

'And well didst thou deserve to.'

As if annihilated by these words the contralto fell back and did not move again. It was obvious that he had drawn his last breath. Tosca too was motionless, rapt in contemplation of the dagger which she still held in her hands, in the attitude of a bride holding her nuptial bouquet. And once again her eyes seemed to me to turn furtively towards the box where I was seated. After a long silence, she sang out:

'In death justice wins,
I forgive him all his sins.'

As she utters these words the hem of her tunic falls slightly aside revealing a narrow foot in the golden thongs of a sandal. She lifts the foot and rests it on the corpse's head, presses it down, and thus remains, triumphant, in her golden tunic, with her mane of hair which falls upon her shoulders like a black cloak, and on her face that drunken, Maenad-like expression. Her macabre enthusiasm is empha-sised by equally triumphant music, in a martial tempo, to which is joined an approaching chorus of men's voices:

'In death justice wins,
let us forgive every sin.'

These were doubtless the liberated prisoners who, led by the beloved husband, would soon erupt on to the stage to congratulate Tosca and celebrate her glory. With a shudder I rose and left the box. The proofs, I thought, would be easily found; mean-while, on the morrow itself, I would give the order to imprison the cavaliere Mario Cavaradossi, creator of the painting *Maria Triumphant*.

The voices kept up their jubilant refrain, fol-lowing me all along the corridor and even into the atrium:

'In death justice wins,
let us forgive every sin.'

Words which I would gladly and wholeheartedly endorse; but their link with Tosca, with the golden tunic and the foot raised to crush the head of the evil one, altered their meaning into a hymn of blas-phemy, into a liturgy, violent and contagious, for a religion I did not wish to know.

IT WOULD SEEM that there is altogether no way of avoiding her; she continues to appear before my eyes as do temptations from the devil, and like these she assumes the most varied forms: at one moment she is the protagonist of the *Triumph of Virtue*, at another the woman dressed in black kneeling at prayer, and finally she is Maria Triumphant with her naked foot crushing the head of the serpent. Since that evening in the theatre, or perhaps earlier, ever since the ill-omened visit to the church, it can be said that there has not been a moment when she is not present in my thoughts. Sometimes she has stepped into the forefront, demanding all my attention for herself, at other times she has loomed in the background, a blurred and yet recognisable figure. In some way or other she was always on stage, and my attempts to bring the curtain down were all in vain. Even my solitude in that quiet of the study was no longer as it had been, but an unwilled and uninterrupted experience of dwelling intimately with that image, a matter of slowly becoming accustomed to it despite all attempts to repel it or erase it.

She now took up so much space in my mind that when I opened the door of the study and saw her sitting in the antechamber I did not believe it could be her in flesh and blood: perhaps the morbid fantasies which were intoxicating me had taken on a corporeal appearance, a spectral substance. Terrified, I banged the double door shut again.

This fear lasted only a moment, of course, scarcely had I acted thus irrationally than I regained my composure. Finding Tosca sitting in my antechamber, I told myself, was much less improbable than finding a ghost there. I looked again, with circumspection, through the spyhole: she was sitting in an armchair, staring at the door, with the expression of a wild beast lying in wait. A red hanging was behind her, against which her figure stood out clearly. She was wearing the very same attire which I had seen her dressed in at the church, and I wondered why she persisted in wearing black, since I knew her to be in no mourning, except the one that I myself had in store for her.

Certainly, her attire seemed to bear out the hypothesis of a materialisation of my obsession; so many times had I brought her to mind like this, head bent over the prie-dieu addressing impious prayers to her own portrait. Yet the woman sitting in the antechamber had a solidity which I would say was incontestable, such as to leave not the slightest doubt about her existence. Moreover from the hem of her skirt there peeped the tip of a small black shoe, a detail which in church I had not noticed. She tapped it rhythmically on the floor, as if giving vent to her own impatience, but that capricious, almost despotic movement was contradicted by the deadly fear which clouded her eyes. Thus she had appeared to me on stage, as the third act began, when she inwardly contemplated the bloody deed with which she must stain her gentle hands.

I could not understand how she had reached me. In my apartment, it needs to be made clear, the antechamber fulfils a purely decorative, or one might say, symbolic function; it is the place wherein would sit whoever waits to be received, if I ever were to consent to receive anyone, and the fact that it is always empty is the visible proof that I do not consent. Those chairs with their pristine upholstery confirm my very inaccessibility, and that was why it pleased me to look upon them. Now instead I shall never more be able to cross the antechamber without my thoughts turning to the unexpected and unbelievable invasion which Tosca has dared to carry out.

Because this was indeed an invasion, neither more nor less; and it was indeed an outrageous impudence with which that woman imposed her presence upon me, this time openly and brutally, rather than through the tortuous paths of memory or imagination. The singer, the lover of the painter, granted herself the right to be there in flesh and blood, just yards away from me, defying all the measures adopted to maintain my isolation. The matter would of course be the subject of a meticulous investigation and those responsible would undergo an exemplary chastisement, but this thought was not enough to

console me; the damage was now done, Tosca occupied the antechamber with the air of someone who
will yield not an inch of conquered ground, and her
gaze resolutely fixed on the door seemed to tell me
that, however long I might be able to resist, shut up
inside the chamber, she would be able to resist much
longer on the outside.

It was precisely this implicit threat that sent me
into a rage. No one can presume to threaten Baron
Scarpia; in terms of the universal order this would
be as if the lamb lay in wait in the undergrowth in
order to ambush the wolf. Alas the comparison was
inappropriate; in Tosca there was nothing that
remotely recalled a lamb, not the slightest trace of
docility, despite the contrary view of the two librettists. Yet, I reflected, I was still Baron Scarpia. A
thought only tautological on the surface, in reality
brimming over with meanings, from which I drew
comfort in the midst of my predicament. It is true,
I thought, that Floria Tosca too is still Floria Tosca,
and perhaps even Cavaradossi's lover, like me, found
in her own name a centre in which to take solid
form, a compendium of her fateful essence, but
Scarpia would get the better of this essence. It would
be irrational to think otherwise.

I therefore stifled the almost superstitious fear
which that woman inspired in me, hid the anger
which still made me tremble beneath the mask of
disdain, and opened the door. Momentarily Tosca
betrayed her own bewilderment before opposing my
mask with an equally impenetrable one of her own.
She smiled, vaguely, as if answering the greeting of
some admirer, but her eyes glittered with anxiety.

'Signorina, to what do I owe the honour?'

'Signore,' she answered, rising, 'I must speak with you at length, privately.'

'As you see, there is not a living soul here, but if you prefer, you can come into my study.'

I showed her in and offered her a chair, the most uncomfortable I could find. She arranged herself in it as if in a soft armchair, leaning lazily against the rigid back.

I moved around the desk and sat down opposite her, some distance away. 'Now have the goodness to tell me the reason for so much secrecy.'

'Obviously Baron Scarpia wishes to make fun of me. Baron Scarpia well knows the reason.'

'If you are referring to the case of that rash young man . . . yes, that nobleman whose name escapes me for the moment. . .'

'I shall remind you of it.'

'Please go no further, I beg you; what does it matter? I attend to so many cases of this kind, and from what I can see each is like the others.'

'But this time, sir, the man is innocent.'

'Of that, young lady, let me be the judge. Besides, I gather that the esteemed cavaliere has fled to escape arrest, and this certainly does not count in favour of his innocence.'

'Even an innocent man can go in fear of your methods.'

'What do you know about my methods?'

'They are on everyone's lips.'

'You too, dear young lady, are on everyone's lips.'

'What do you mean by that?'

'That your reputation as a pious and virtuous woman is so great as to have reached even me in my refuge here. For this reason, you see, it amazes me somewhat to hear you intercede on behalf of a man of so doubtful a reputation, and of whom, what is more, you are not even a relative.'

'Are family ties then necessary that one might strive for innocence to triumph?'

'If I am not mistaken, you have a singular fondness for the word "triumph" and its derivatives. Consider, I beg you, that a warrant for imprisonment has already been issued against that individual.'

'In other words, you have issued it.'

'It has been issued, I repeat, by that superior form of justice which I unworthily represent.'

'Justice can sometimes be mistaken, and likewise also its representatives.'

'Do you really believe that in matters of such importance the Lord abandons us to our human fallibility? No, dear Tosca, He will always guide the thoughts of whoever serves Him to perceive the true, and the hand to carry out the good. For this reason, you see, when I find myself up there carrying out my humble duty it seems to me that I am closer to His infinite majesty than at any other time, as if I were thereby practising a special kind of praying, I should venture to say of mystic ecstasy.'

'In your view, then, God would command us to torture our neighbours?'

'I remind you, since your manner of living seems to have led you to forget it, that He exhorts us to mortify the flesh.'

'Ours, however, not that of others.'

'The sex to which you belong excuses the lack of logic in your argument. But why should it be, I ask you, that in order to please the Lord, mortification should necessarily be carried out upon one's own person? Are not perhaps all creatures linked by some obscure sympathy, by a common origin and substance which allows each of us to be reflected in the suffering of others, to recognise in it one's own fragility and wretchedness?'

'Can it be you who speaks of sympathy ... when sympathy should lead to compassion?'

'And who tells you, may I ask, that I feel no compassion?'

She answered with an offensive, sneering laugh. 'Your skill in hiding it is truly remarkable.'

'And yet, dear young lady, it is precisely compassion that guides my hand, the sympathy to which I was referring. Without it, upstairs, when I interrogate the condemned, I could not fulfil my duty with the right amount of zeal, I would not have the invigorating knowledge of punishing in them that corrupt nature of which alas I also have a part.'

'It is a vicious circle.'

'If it pleases you, then define it thus. Unfortunately, between ourselves, it is a rather short circle. The majority of the suspects do not display the least capacity for tolerating pain, so that the interrogations are always over, one way or another, within forty minutes. Who knows, perhaps your friend will demonstrate a greater talent, but personally I doubt it. How else can it be, experience has made me sceptical. Nowadays the vocation for martyrdom is becoming increasingly rare, even in its profane forms.'

'I did not know that a special vocation was needed to be tortured.'

'You smile at my theories,' I answered, even though she was really not smiling at all, and as she listened to me she had grown paler still. 'And yet without that talent only mediocre, aesthetically unsatisfying results are obtained. Yes, dear young lady, however strange it may seem to you, there is also an aesthetic of torture, just as there is a particular genius, as much on the part of the victim as on the part of the bloodletter.'

'And you are without doubt a genius in your profession.'

'I admit it without any false modesty. But victims of genius, in truth, have never yet come my way.'

I cannot say why I had yielded to the impulse to elaborate these thoughts of mine to her, which usually I kept jealousy to myself, without putting them into words, not even with my spiritual director. What could Floria Tosca understand of the aesthetic of torture, or of the ten categories under which, in a short, well-ordered treatise, I had tried to group its tangible manifestations? What could she understand of the rigid moral and intellectual discipline implicit in every form of torment? Yet, when I turned my gaze towards her, I seemed to glimpse in her dark eyes a faint glimmer of understanding, a certain curiosity which I felt inclined to satisfy.

'Listen to these sounds, these groans; right above our heads is a room of which many things are told, but only on hearsay, because I and my men leave that room with our lips sealed, and the others, the suspects, do not leave it at all, or else only to keep an appointment with the firing squad. The walls of that room are padded, so that the screams do not escape. You know, they would disturb my concentration.'

She stared at me as if mesmerised. 'Will the cavaliere be taken up there?'

I nodded. 'Alas, young lady, I shall not be able to repay your kindness; in Paradise, that is the name we give it among ourselves, there are no boxes and the presence of an audience is not allowed.'

'You speak as though he were already in your hands.'

'As do you, it appears. Yet, believe me, it is only a matter of time.'

'Is there really no hope of persuading you? I thought, dear Baron, that you had consented to let me speak of him, to plead his cause. . .'

I was not won over by this suddenly subordinate behaviour, this wheedling demeanour; I had already seen its very like when watching the third act of the *Triumph of Virtue*.

'In other words you thought,' I said severely, 'that if you could speak to me in tête à tête, without witnesses, for instance in the privacy of a study or a little temple in Corinthian style, you would manage to persuade me to change my mind.'

Her eyes became hard, her voice harsh. 'Off-stage, sir, Floria Tosca is not in the habit of proposing bargains of that kind.'

'Come now, do not upset yourself. Obviously, I

have misinterpreted your words. So let us allow justice to follow its course, unbending as is its nature.'

'If I were to beseech you, in the name of that God worshipped by us both. . .'

'And by you, dear young lady, so ill-served. I beg you, do not utter His name before me, on your lips it sounds like blasphemy. You are too taken up with yourself to know any other god but your vanity.'

'And you, sir, give His name to your wickedness, to your thirst for blood.'

She had leapt to her feet, and I did likewise. We looked at one another in silence for a few moments, like that afternoon in church, beside the holy water font.

'Be seated, Tosca, I did not wish to offend you. If I presumed to speak to you harshly, it was with the most brotherly of intentions.'

'You have already painted me a clear enough picture of your brotherly love,' she retorted, while nonetheless taking a seat once more.

'It is susceptible to misapprehensions, I admit, yet when you know me better. . .'

'Do you really suppose that I wish to deepen our acquaintance?'

'I suppose that you wish to help the cavaliere Cavaradossi.'

'It would seem that you now recall his name.'

'Persistent rumour links it with your own. And sarcasm, dear young lady, does not become the position in which you find yourself. After all, you are here to make an appeal to my clemency, to my generosity. . .'

'I have been naive, dear baron. I thought you a man.'

'A man like the rest, you mean? Like those over whom you are used to exercise your feminine tyranny?'

'Like those able to feel pity for the misfortunes of his neighbour.'

'Well, tell the cavaliere to be so good as to give himself up; I will have every opportunity to pity him during the interrogations. And were these to result in his innocence, believe me, I should be the first to rejoice.'

'So it only remains for me to take my leave,' she said, rising once more. I was glad of her decision to terminate that encounter, by which I felt exhausted as if from some long battle. I went to the door and opened it for her.

On the threshold Tosca extended a hand, which I bent to kiss. 'Forgive me, baron, if I have taken you away from your affairs.'

'On the contrary, Signorina; it has been a real pleasure to speak with you.'

And at heart I did not lie, even if the nature of that pleasure was quite other than soothing. Throughout the whole interview, as Tosca sat opposite me, I seemed to find myself upon a layer of ice under which the oceans heaved unseen, and at certain moments I had feared the ice would break. This is why as soon as I had closed the door at her back and was alone in my study, I experienced the immense relief of someone feeling dry land once more safe and sound beneath his feet.

A FEW DAYS HAVE gone by since Tosca's visit and still, as I glance through dossiers or write out warrants for imprisonment, I often catch myself listening out in the silence which surrounds me, whether in hope or in fear I cannot say, for the sound of those little black shoes tapping on the floor. At the least noise, a creak, the rustle of a curtain stirred by the breeze, I rush to the door to look through the spyhole into the empty antechamber.

Sooner or later she must return, but this time not through her own initiative; I will be the one to summon her, with a written order or an invitation of a less official character, but just as peremptory. It is indeed up to me to set the rules, and for her to have usurped this privilege of mine is something very grave, intolerable, which demands a response of the utmost severity.

She dared to proclaim herself a fellow believer; I shall therefore instruct her in the arduous path of true belief, convince her that those mortal coils, that flesh in whose ephemeral splendour she takes such pleasure are in reality suffering and wretchedness and the living tomb of the soul.

I shall teach her all this with recourse to the faculty of imagination, which is admittedly, as I have already had occasion to say, a tool of the devil and a perpetual hotbed of evil, but also a powerful didactic aid for those who wish to escape from evil. It is a widespread practice among spiritual directors to guide the penitent to imagine, in the most vivid manner, the torments of hell, depicted with all the colours of reality, so that the soul, terrified by this vision, will flee from sin; through my female disciple's imagination I shall show instead the torments of Paradise, and I am confident of producing thus the same effect.

Besides, I have myself undertaken to pursue such an itinerary, the better to defend myself from the enticements which the beautiful sight of that woman could exert on my senses. In the morning as soon as I get up, and then again at night before I go to bed, and also in the course of the day if the memory of her becomes too insistent, I apply myself faithfully and methodically to a purifying exercise which consists in representing to myself the lineaments of Floria Tosca gradually deformed by old age, by death, and by corruption, until they dissolve into that dust from which we all come and to which we shall return. Little by little, beneath her seductive outer covering I manage plainly to discern the nakedness of the skeleton, and at the sight of this I feel both a great pity and a great relief. Whosoever can keep his eye fixed boldly and unwaveringly upon the transcience and fragility of earthly things will thereby attain an unlimited power over them; the spirit is no longer shadowed by the veils of the mortal condition that shroud it, but becomes, inasmuch as is possible, akin to its Creator. The world's glories, its riches, the lures of the senses, all thereafter becomes subordinate: thus the eagle in his untramelled flight holds sway over the highest peaks, dominating them and at the same time making them his.

One more week of these exercises and I shall be able to meet Floria Tosca again without feeling the slightest unease. For now, a visit from her would be premature; this was confirmed for me last night, when to put myself to the test I made my way to that well-known church.

This time Holy Mass was in progress attended by a few gaunt old women. With half an eye I regarded the black figures bent over the pews in the central nave; as for them, I thought, there is little left for the imagination to do, nature has already taken due care to mark the intimations of mortality. But from the Attavanti chapel, Maria Triumphant, illumined by candles, exuberant with life and with beauty, turned her ambiguous smile upon me.

I tried to concentrate my attention on the words of the liturgy spoken by the priest, yet they reached me from a distance, as if mass were being celebrated in one world and I were in another, an outlandish and disturbing one, whose borders were precisely those described by the thick golden frame around the canvas of the painting. Only three inhabitants dwelt on that secret planet: I, the serpent and the womanly figure with the raven-black mane, in which for sure I did not discern the Virgin intent on crushing the head of Satan, but a character of much greater profanity, depicted at the moment of sealing a deadly pact with him.

The woman seemed to look towards me, inviting me, in that Eden already infected with evil, to play the willing part of Adam; I however had chosen a quite different role for myself, the office of Michael, the vengeful archangel, and in my heart I attested an utter loyalty to that office, while around me the pious females repeated the words of the priest, transforming them into a rise and fall of senseless murmurings.

When mass was over they shuffled out of the church. The celebrant had withdrawn, the sacristan was extinguishing the candles one by one and directed inquisitive glances towards me. I feigned to be absorbed in prayer, but my stealthy eyes followed him when he entered the Attavanti chapel, and I watched the blaze of the candles grow dim and the great canvas above the altar become darker and darker and more indistinct.

At last I remained alone. For a moment I imagined Floria Tosca lurking in the darkness of the chapel, waiting for me to take a step towards her. Then I rose, and slowly I approached the painting.

FLORIA TOSCA visited me again yesterday, on the day of Our Lady of Sorrows, late in the afternoon. When I asked her how she had managed once more to reach me without being announced, she answered that she had found the great door open and that it had only taken a somewhat modest tip to ensure that the doorkeeper's attention conveniently wandered. 'So it is not so difficult,' she concluded, 'to enter this building.'

'What matters,' I retorted, 'is that it is difficult to leave it. As for the doorkeeper, rest assured: he will be punished for his venality.'

She lowered her eyelids. 'My visit is therefore so displeasing?'

'That is not what I meant.'

I led her into the study and without waiting for any sign from me she made herself comfortable in the chair which she had occupied the time before. I was about to do likewise, moving to the other side of the desk, but Tosca stopped me by gripping my arm.

'Come, sit here next to me,' she said with a smile. Do not be afraid.'

'Afraid, signorina?'

'Of the feminine tyranny which you think I can so well exert.'

I could not but return her smile and obey her, yet that proximity made me uneasy, as did the excessively familiar manner which she had adopted. Not even when I was seated did she let go of my arm, but kept a hand resting on it, as if absentmindedly. Obviously she had decided to change tactics, the proud champion of misjudged innocence had become a fragile woman in need of protection.

That surrender, I felt instinctively, was rather more fearsome than the contempt displayed in the earlier interview, and yet it could be turned to useful ends of my own. I decided therefore to play along and exhibit fatherly indulgence.

'I too,' I said edging away unobtrusively so as to compel her to let go of my arm, 'hope that I did not frighten you too much the other day.'

'If it were so, dear baron, it would in any case be in your power to reassure me.'

'I should do so with pleasure. But you see, he whom you have before you is merely the humble servant of a higher will.'

'Indeed? Yet I thought you were supposed to be a genius, a master in command of his art.'

'The one, dear young lady, does not exclude the other. To serve, to command... How could it be possible to separate these ideas?'

'Forgive me, I am a poor ignorant woman, I am

unable to understand how two opposing ideas can be inseparable.'

'You will understand when you learn to dominate yourself, to restrain your passions.'

'To serve whom?'

'The Lord whom we all should serve devotedly.'

'Ah, I should be happy to. But, surely you are forgetting that I am too taken up with myself to know any other god but my vanity.'

'Come, do not despair: there is a cure for everything.'

'Besides, excuse me, I cannot grasp the connection between my capacity to serve and the safety of Cavaradossi.'

'Cavaradossi!' I exclaimed in exasperation. 'It seems that you can think of nothing else.'

'He has helped me, he has shown himself to be devoted. . .'

'And he has been well rewarded for it, from what I have heard. But one day, dear young lady, it will be your turn to appear before a supreme Tribunal, and on that day the good Cavaradossi, for all his help and devotion, will be unable to do anything to save you.'

'Whereas Baron Scarpia imagines that he can do something?'

'Not a great deal, let it be understood, but perhaps in all these years some morsel of credit has come to be mine.'

'Without a doubt; the God of love, the God of mercy, must take great satisfaction in watching, from up there, the good works which you carry out in your Paradise.'

'I flatter myself in believing it so, signorina.'

'In any case, that day is still far off, and if meanwhile you can do me the courtesy of not digressing. . .'

'Digressing? How can you accuse me of digressing when the subject to which I referred is the only truly important one for every mortal creature? Or would you wish to place above it an obscure nobleman who attempts to emerge from obscurity by conspiring against the law and subjecting others to his painter's whims?'

'Everyone, dear baron, expresses his own talents in the art most congenial to himself. Doubtless you will have had the opportunity to see the cavaliere's paintings.'

'Certainly not. At least, not as far as I recall.'

'And yet I thought I glimpsed you, a few weeks ago, in front of the canvas representing the Holy Virgin in the church of . . .'

'Precisely,' I said roughly, 'I happened to visit that church, for professional reasons, and if I am not mistaken I also had the honour of seeing you there, albeit fleetingly. But as far as the picture you speak of . . . the Holy Virgin, you said? No, I really don't remember it.'

'Perhaps you did not notice it. The church, besides, was dark.'

'Very dark. And alas my eyesight is no longer what it was. Old age, dear signorina, makes no allowances for anyone, it even dares threaten Baron Scarpia.'

'Old age!' she repeated, placing a hand on my arm once again. 'Do you wish to make fun of me?

That a man such as you, still so fascinating, should abandon himself to these melancholy thoughts. . .'

'Do you deem them melancholy? I cannot see why. I have certainly not placed the meaning of my life in the vigour of the body.'

'And yet the exercise of your art must require considerable physical powers.'

'Rather less than that of the painter. These days there are greatly refined systems, thanks to which a minimum of energy will obtain really quite extraordinary effects. And then, of course, I entrust the more menial and tiresome tasks to others; mine is a predominantly spiritual office, of supervision and management. Nonetheless I do not deny that sometimes I have been pleased to intervene even in the material aspect, as perhaps your friend Cavaradossi takes pleasure in mixing his colours himself.'

'What counts however are the finishing touches,' she said, 'the hand of the master.'

I pretended not to notice her sarcasm. 'Precisely, signorina; from what I can see we understand one another perfectly. These touches, to go back to your fine image, are present and recognisable in everything which is carried out up there.'

'But no one can recognise it. It is a matter of a secret art, bereft of an audience.'

'It would be more accurate to define it as an art in which the audience participates in the work, and does not outlive it.'

'I understand. So the victim, in the short time allowed to him, would be the only person who could measure your talent, your mastery. But then, dear baron, you would need someone able to appreciate both of these as deserved, and good Cavaradossi is certainly no expert.'

'What alternative would you suggest?'

She removed her fingers from my arm. 'It seems to me that the metaphor has gone too far.'

'It seems likewise to me.'

She rose and went over to a window. She stood there motionless for a few moments, with her back turned to me, and finally opened the curtain. Daylight suddenly invaded the room.

'It is better like this, do you not find? By the sun's illumination thoughts too become clearer.'

'I prefer the shadow, but if you wish you may leave it open; poor girl, do you have need of cheer? Perhaps you would like a goblet of Spanish wine?'

'Thank you, do not trouble yourself.'

'I too would gladly sip some to keep you company.'

She turned towards me. 'It is late, I must go.'

'The sun, as you see, is still high; you could stay a little longer and have plenty of time to reach the theatre. My carriage, of course, is at your disposal.'

'Thank you, but I must go.'

'What are you afraid of?'

She fixed her eyes upon mine, without answering, and then lowered her gaze.

'Not of me, I hope,' I said kindly, 'I have never given you any reason to fear me. On the contrary, it seems to me that I have always shown the utmost benevolence towards you.'

'I am grateful to you. However, you have always avoided the real reason for my visits.'

'The real reason? And you are sure you know it?'

'If you wish I can tell you it again.'

'There is no need, I know very well what you would say. But sometimes, you know, the ends which we believe we pursue are not the true ones. Sometimes a superior will uses us to lead us where we do not mean to go, and where nonetheless a great reward awaits us.'

'Or a great punishment,' she murmured.

'Who can foretell?'

'Reward, punishment... You will maintain, I imagine, that it is not possible to separate these ideas completely.'

'It is a fundamental truth, signorina, and I listen to it with a joy that is all the greater for it coming from your lips, not mine.'

'It comforts me to feel I have the good opinion of a man of such great learning.'

'And how could I not have a good opinion of you? Already you seem no longer the same woman who came here three days ago with that arrogant demeanour, with that contempt for the authority that I so unworthily . . .'

'Three days ago, you said?'

'Three or four,' I answered with embarrassment. 'I cannot say precisely, I have certainly not been counting. You will understand, my days are crowded with engagements, and one visit among so many, however greatly welcome. . . I shall gladly arrange a new appointment for you as soon as I have some time.'

'When do you think you can? Because, you see, my days too are crowded with engagements.'

'You have caught me unprepared, dear Tosca, I

must first consult my secretary. I shall have a note sent to you.'

'Excellent. And should the bearer not find me at home, order that it be given to my maid.'

'A woman so worldly and she still trusts maids?'

'Why should I not trust them?'

'Because often they read their master's correspondence.'

'And what of it? It does not seem to me that what goes between us should demand any special secrecy.'

'No, you are right.'

She hesitated at the door, which I had opened for her.

'I hope then, dear signorina, soon to have the pleasure of seeing you again.'

When I took her hand to bring it to my lips, I felt it tremble once again with that faint tremor, proudly restrained and yet invincible, with which she had received the holy water from me in church. This time, however, not even my own hands were altogether steady.

IN RECENT DAYS I have done nothing but devote myself to my pedagogical mission. An important part of this was represented by the purchase of the bracelet, a strange bracelet destined, had I not fortuitously discovered it, to remain forever in the goldsmith's shop; it was in fact bereft of any decoration, a simple circlet of gold which, except for its material, was like those attached to the walls of Paradise and clamped around the prisoners' wrists when necessary. It was this very resemblance which induced me to purchase it, there and then convincing me that I would never find a more appropriate present.

That very evening I made my way to the theatre, taking with me the bracelet enclosed in an elegant box, in order to deliver it personally to Floria Tosca. When I arrived the curtain had already come down some time since and I feared that she would by now have gone home; yet she had stayed on in her dressing-room, no longer in costume, to no apparent purpose. Had she perhaps remained at the theatre to wait for me? I felt the idea arouse a singular excitement.

Tosca too seemed troubled, although she made a show of being unperturbed. Her dressing-room was at the end of a long corridor and she was seated in front of the dressing-table with her back to the door, which she had left open. Without a doubt she could see my image reflected in the mirror, but she did not turn; she remained quite motionless, her posture however assuming an unnatural rigidity.

I crossed the threshold of the dressing-room and greeted her. Only then, feigning surprise, did she decide to turn towards me.

'Ah, Baron Scarpia! I had no idea that you would come to pay me a visit.'

Quick-eyed as she was, she had immediately noticed the box I held in my hand, and cast childishly covetous looks upon it. I however did not give her the present at once, preferring to let her curiosity grow.

'I am here, of course, to pay my compliments,' I said with a slight bow, 'but also to remind you of your engagement.'

'Which engagement?'

'To come back and see me when I summon you.'

'I shall certainly come, one of these days.'

'I repeat, signorina: when I summon you. You see there is nothing I loathe more in the world than unexpected visits, and you would certainly not be acting for the good of the cavaliere by contravening my wishes once again.'

'Are you so sure that I will obey you?'

'Every creature, dear signorina, naturally inclines

to their own interest, and at this moment it is in your interest to obey me. Assuming that it still really matters to you to save one known to us from a wretched fate.'

She did not answer. She gave the mirror a sidelong look, as if to reassure herself that her own image had not changed in the meantime. 'Do take a seat,' she said, then pointed to an armchair next to hers.

I sat down and placed the box on the dressing-table, around which there lingered the fragrance of cosmetics. The same intense, dizzying fragrance emanated from Tosca's person, making her body, though so close, strangely inaccessible, like a planet clothed in its own atmosphere.

I pushed the box towards her.

'Is this for me? What a kind thought!'

'A trifle, a small sign of my friendship.'

Impatiently she took hold of the container, opened it and removed the bracelet. She seemed struck, whether pleasurably or unpleasurably, by its severity of form. 'A kind thought indeed,' she said turning the piece of jewellery around in her hands.

'So why not try it on?'

She hesitated for a moment, then held it out to me. 'Put it on for me.'

She extended her arm towards me and I clasped the circlet of gold around her wrist. When I closed it, locking the catch, I saw that it sank just slightly into her flesh.

'It is too tight,' she protested.

'Yet it seems to me that it fits you wonderfully.'

'It seems to you?' said Tosca angrily. She took it off and began inspecting her wrist, around which the bracelet had outlined two fine red circles. 'See for yourself: it is an instrument of torture.'

'I have never maintained otherwise,' I retorted coldly. 'Did you perhaps expect that Scarpia was preparing a bed of roses for you?'

'Were you to give me a rose I should at once look for the thorns.'

'A crown of thorns, you should know, is a reward much higher than a crown of roses. Too high, I fear, for one like you.'

'Then keep it; let it not be that I should aspire to an honour of which I am unworthy.'

Once more she pushed the bracelet towards me but I was careful not to take it back.

'Do not imagine, sir, that I have failed to understand what lies behind this.'

'The perfecting of your nature, signorina, and nothing more. It grieves me that you find my charity so displeasing.'

'You of all people dare to speak of charity?'

'I of all people, of course. Your greatest sin is pride, but who else could free you from it?'

'Meaning,' she said with a quick nervous laugh, 'that I am to go to you to learn humility.'

'If you have not been able to learn it even in church I fear that no other means is left.'

'Scarpia the villain, Scarpia the tyrant, would therefore be an elevated soul, moved solely by love of his neighbour.'

'That is just so. Or do you deceive yourself that all this gives me some pleasure? I am a very busy man, signorina, I bear an office of great importance and responsibility, and yet I waste my time with you in this sordid place. . .'

She leapt to her feet. 'I shall not make you waste any more time. I entreat you to take back this small sign of your friendship and consider yourself dismissed for once and all.'

That fury and arrogance affected me deeply. 'The loveliest flower, the most pleasing to the Lord, is humility when it blooms within a prideful soul. But you kneel only before yourself, before your sublime person.'

'If you hope to see me on my knees before you, you will have to wait a while.'

'Well, signorina, I congratulate you. Continue then on this road of yours and much good may it do you.'

'And you continue too on yours; I shall certainly not come to beg the wolf to spare the lamb.'

'I invite you however to recall that the wolf came one day to you in the spirit of brotherhood and offered you salvation.'

'I am grateful to you for the thought, but I can look to my salvation by myself.'

'As well we have seen. The great care you take of your soul is on everyone's lips. You are concerned no longer now with Cavaradossi's fate, another obviously has taken his place.'

She was shaking, such was her indignation. 'I ask you once more to go.'

I went on my way, but I left the bracelet on the dressing-table, plain to be seen; there always remained the possibility, however remote, that on more mature reflection Tosca might put it on again.

Beneath a clouded sky through which the white sickle of the moon was barely visible I made my way back with hurried steps. No sound could be heard, although from a few half-open shutters there still dimly shone some light upon the empty streets. The air was heavy, with not the faintest breeze to shake it from its torpor, and in that stillness the perfumes of the plants became oppressive and intense, like the fragrances surrounding Tosca in her dressing-room. A crown of thorns is a higher reward than a crown of roses, the loveliest flower is humility when it blooms within the prideful soul; these words kept returning to my mind, and there returned to my mind the slender wrist marked with the two red circles which Tosca had showed me in an unwitting promise.

If she suspected me of impure motives this grieved me, but it did not amaze me; like, I thought, knows only like, and a corrupt creature, wherever her eye might turn will perceive only corruption. Thus the unhappy woman instinctively placed me on a level with the wretched humanity she had until then moved among, misinterpreting the generous impulse which impelled me, while I could discern in her the sublime flame of sacrifice and abnegation, despite all the arrogance in which she cloaked herself. The very intensity of her will was guarantee of an equal intensity in her submission to the will of another, it made her potentially the most devoted servant of the Lord. And the way of obedience to the Lord was of course the usual one, the ladder of hierarchy, in keeping with the universal order, in which my unworthy person represented the first rung.

And yet I realised with dismay that my imagination came to a satisfying halt upon that rung and seemed tempted to remain there. If that flower of humility were ever to bloom in that prideful soul, mine would be the first hand to pluck it and would I not then have yielded to the impulse to hold it, to keep it for myself? Although I knew that I was moved by better intentions, I was tormented by the most agonising scruples and the most cruel suspicions.

I had almost arrived when I heard the sound of a carriage in the distance. I thought it was coming in my direction and I hid behind the columns of a portico, like he who fears discovery by unknown eyes while he is engaged in some villainous occupation. But the carriage turned before it reached me, the sound of hooves and creaking wheels gradually fading away into the silence of the night, until I could no longer hear them. Then I left my hiding place and went on my way again.

With a sigh of relief I reached the portal of my house and once inside I hastened to lock it with triple bolts, almost as if I believed I could leave outside, beyond the heavy double doors, Floria Tosca and everything concerning her. On the stairs all at once I was gripped with a desire to climb up to Paradise and remain there for some time in solitude among those familiar instruments, in that place crowded with memories dear to me. But suddenly I realised that it was not just the memories that drew me there, but some unfathomable hope, by which I felt myself overcome without being able to understand its true nature. As a precaution, I resolutely forebade myself that visit; I would go to Paradise when the time came, neither sooner nor later, and only in order to carry out my office with the greatest sobriety.

When I entered my study I saw a paper on the desk; it was an official document reporting the disappearance of a painting. *Maria Triumphant*, to be precise, oil on canvas by Mario Cavaradossi, previously held in the chapel of the Attavanti family and now having mysteriously vanished from it. This was suspected to be a sacrilegious act of theft by some Jacobin or other. It seems, I thought with a smile, that Cavaradossi and his accomplices will have to account also for this.

But at that moment the image of Maria Triumphant appeared to me with clarity, almost as if I had it before my eyes; the pale white wrists were folded crosswise on her breast and I saw that they were marked with fine red circles. I fervently hoped that Tosca would hold true to her threats and never return.

DAYS OF ANGUISH followed that interview. I stayed
in my study with the door locked, unable to bring
myself to look through the spyhole to the antechamber. I had even, it shames me to say so, stopped
my visits to Paradise and I peremptorily ordered my
men not to disturb me except for grave reasons. Not
even at night did I quit that hiding place; to sleep I
made a bed as best I could on a couch or just on
the hard marble floor. Physical suffering might
perhaps have availed me forgiveness for my sins, but
I sought it out most of all in the rather more profane
hope of stifling the thoughts that assailed me.

Sometimes I would go to a window, the same one
which Tosca had approached during her last visit,
and like her I drew aside the curtains, but without
opening them completely; I merely parted them and
if it was in the day I would close them abruptly
again, for the light of the sun caused me pain. At
night, however, I would stay for a while watching
the sky, the outlines of buildings which stood out
plainly by the light of the moon, which now was

high and pale, now very very near, as if skimming the roofs with its fiery red mass. This unexpected nearness and lofty distance alike exerted a powerful fascination upon me, and often, heedless of the time that went by, I would remain at the window to follow every phase of the gradual progress from one to the other. When the moon drew near with its flaming hues I felt oppressed and wished only to see it vanish into distant skies, but once it reached them and had grown faint, transparent and almost evanescent I should have liked to keep it in my field of sight indefinitely. As soon as it had disappeared completely, abandoning me to the deep, dark vastness of the night, solitude no longer seemed to me a comfort and protection, but a bitter sentence. Then I would draw the curtains close again and turn back into the room, on which the foggy candlelight conferred an aspect just as desolate.

Since my contemplation of the landscape gave me no relief, impelling me to those thoughts from which I would wish to flee, one evening, seeking a distraction, I started to go through my papers. The first dossier which fell under my eyes was the one relating to Mario Cavaradossi. Revolted, I put down the file again. I opened another and came across the report of the disappearance of *Maria Triumphant*. So as to avoid all inopportune associations I decided to look through the documents of past years, reviewing my career and lingering over its most brilliant episodes; for example the arrest of the violinist whom women idolised. At once however I recalled that the art of the violin was akin to that of singing, and that between a man idolised by women and a woman idolised by men there existed a displeasing mirror relation. But how different, I thought bitterly, had been my bearing on that occasion, when I had boldly entered the hall to interrupt the concert, from that hasty flight from the theatre during the third act of *The Triumph of Virtue*! I asked myself if Baron Scarpia was still Baron Scarpia, armed with unassailable severity and viewed by the whole city with a fearful respect. Perhaps in the time intervening something had crept into me, some insidious poison gradually sapping my energies; perhaps in church, brushing Tosca's hand to give her the holy water, I had received in exchange that ruinous present. And I remembered Hercules, the strongest of the ancient heroes, who horribly and slowly was consumed imprisoned in the centaur's tunic.

And yet, I told myself, this poison's effects would with time be lessened if I did not see Tosca again. In this respect our last conversation left me hopeful; my small gift had provoked in her an outrage such that she would not easily consent to meet me again. I thought she would have thrown away the bracelet in a fit of anger, and with it any chance of saving Cavaradossi. In a woman of her kind, I reflected, pride is destined to prevail over compassion and even over the desire to rescue the man who is beloved. Besides, the intelligence with which she was endowed placed her far above her sex, hence she would by now have been persuaded of the utter uselessness of any efforts to this purpose.

So almost certainly I would never see her again. Through the half-open curtain my study was overlooked by an empty sky, from which even the last star had departed.

I fell asleep as day began to dawn. Usually my slumber is blind, or at the most impinged upon by broken images between which on waking I am unable to perceive any kind of connection. That night however, or rather, that morning, I had a dream of absolute coherence, a manner of brief story in which I myself was the protagonist.

I was to go to the theatre, presumably invited by Floria Tosca, to see *The Triumph of Virtue*. I felt particularly pleased because the key of the royal box had been given to me. Everyone, I thought, would see me, and they would realise the position Baron Scarpia held in the world. Even the equipage which awaited me at the portal to take me to the opera, a sumptuous team of four black-mantled Arab horses, was worthy of a cardinal or prince of the blood. Four lackeys stood beside the carriage, adorned with precious stuccoed work, and when they saw me they bowed silently with the utmost deference, and in this continuing silence handed me inside.

The interior was upholstered in a deep purple velvet. Through the windows the streets I traversed seemed blurred as in a pastel drawing, the angles of the buildings softened, fountains and statues faintly outlined in a golden mist. The slow trotting of the horses set the carriage in a rocking motion to which I gave myself up with happy indolence.

I was aware of having arrived only when a lackey opened the door. Hardly had I stepped down when the carriage made off and I turned to see in front of me the façade of the theatre, all illuminated, with the great doors wide open, although there was not a living soul about and no carriages were parked in the square.

The atrium too was empty, and there too the lights shone down with prodigality. Not seeing any ushers, I ascended the staircase alone and entered the circular corridor from which the boxes were reached. From the auditorium there came the muffled voice of a woman; I recognised it at once. She sang a melody which from time to time I recognised, at other times could only guess, distant and inviting, filled with lengthy silences.

With my key I unlocked the door of the royal box and found myself before a curtain. However hard I tried, I could not succeed in opening it; although it was soft to the touch and apparently yielding, every attempt to move it met the resistance of a wall of steel. Meanwhile the melody continued, remote and enticing, but now it seemed to me I glimpsed in it a subtle mockery.

Finally an usher approached. He looked me up and down with hostile, even scornful eyes, to the point where I suspected I had ventured out in attire unsuitable for the occasion. But it only took a swift inspection of my person to reassure me: I wore the most elegant of formal dress and I had even pinned to my tail-coat a pair of decorations which not a few were envious of.

'My good man,' I said therefore in a haughty tone, 'open that curtain.'

'Why should I open it?' he retorted insolently.

'Because I wish to enter the box.'

'The royal box, you?'

'The royal box, I.'

'And who might you be, may I ask?'

I stared at him without replying. For some reason which now I can no longer comprehend, but which in the dream seemed absolutely logical, I understood I could in no wise utter my own name.

The usher turned his back on me and departed, vanishing almost immediately behind the corridor's curve. Although there was no longer the least sound issuing from the auditorium, I was sure that the voice had not stopped singing; but I was equally sure that it would no longer be vouchsafed me to hear it. Before the usher returned to drive me away, of my own accord I set out towards the exit.

PERHAPS IT WAS indeed that dream which suggested to me, or compelled me rather, to see Tosca; in order to regain energy and serenity I had to assure myself at all costs that it did not correspond to the truth, that she had not been placed out of my reach. At the same time I was daunted by the thought of having another of those conversations with her from which I always emerged exhausted and unnerved. Instead of setting my mind at rest this would have increased my unease.

But fortunately there was an extremely simple way of seeing her without being forced to speak to her: to go to the theatre without warning and watch the performance. Certainly, the wish to keep my identity secret would mean giving up hope of entering the royal box, at least in this the dream showed itself to be prophetic. And if the usher did not recognise me I could only but be glad of it; otherwise, Tosca would be apprised of my presence and would have interpreted it as a sign of weakness and surrender.

I went to the theatre on foot, not only for fear that someone might observe my carriage, but also to avoid displeasing comparisons between it and the luxurious equipage in the dream. Besides, I had myself believe, exercise and fresh air would clear my mind of any unwholesome imaginings.

A light breeze blew over the city, giving all things a clear precise outline and making even the furthest reaches of the landscape peculiarly close and immediate, as if there was nothing in the world which I could not have touched had I only stretched out a hand. Even the sky was bereft of depth. From up there, I thought, God need not make much effort to read in our hearts; and instinctively I stepped to one side of the road in order to walk close to the wall.

This was, moreover, not the only gaze from which I was anxious to remove myself. When I reached the square where the theatre was I saw a group of noblemen in front of the entrance, and among these I thought I recognised a highly placed functionary to whom, some months before, I had gone in order to obtain certain confidential information. I was not sure that he was indeed the one, but I deemed it more prudent to let him go in before I crossed the square. At last, as God wished it, the group dispersed, yet, my relief turned out to be premature; as I was about to reach the portico a carriage halted just some steps away from me and out of it there came the marchesa Attavanti together with a younger woman. She noticed me immediately and I had to approach her to pay my respects.

'Dear marchesa, what an unexpected pleasure,' I said, bringing her ring-laden hand to my lips.

'It is rather more unexpected to meet you: I did not know you were a lover of the opera.'

'Indeed, I cannot abide it. I am here for reasons ... which I am not permitted to reveal.'

'Reasons of office?' she asked excitedly.

I nodded solemnly. 'I am counting, of course, upon your discretion.'

'It goes without saying, dear friend. Besides, even had I wished to be indiscreet, you have so far given me very little of substance.'

'Nothing would please me more than to confide in you, but were I to do so I should be neglecting my duty.'

'Of course, you are forgiven. But my apologies, I almost forgot to introduce you to my niece, the younger daughter of the late lamented Giovanni Maria.'

I respectfully acknowledged the niece, a tall, bony woman of around thirty, whose status of poor relation seemed, instead of humility, to have induced an almost rude lack of manners.

'And such loveliness, dear marchesa, you have kept hidden from us for so long! Affection obviously makes you selfish.'

'Come now, baron, my niece is a simple girl, she is unused to such compliments. And, between ourselves, nor does she merit them. More to the point, tell me, where is your box?'

'As I explained, I am unaccustomed to going to the theatre, and as a consequence I do not even have a box at my disposal.'

'You really are an eccentric fellow. I hope you will do me the honour of coming to mine.'

Unable to refuse, I entered the theatre in the wake of aunt and niece. Thus my clandestine visit acquired the maximum amount of advertisement, with a procession of acquaintances coming up to greet me and subjecting me to close questioning about what had brought me to that place. To these enquiries, which I skilfully avoided, the marchesa took it upon herself to reply by means of hints and allusions, looking around before she spoke, in the manner of a conspirator, while the niece cast me such surly looks that I doubted whether my pretext had successfully convinced her. It is hard for me to say what irritated me the most, whether the interminable chatter of the one or the peevish silence of the other, or having to admit to myself that I was to blame for finding myself in such a regrettable situation as this. The fact that I had come punctually to the theatre and not, as prudence would have suggested, after the start of the performance, struck me as a worrisome symptom of mental confusion. Baron Scarpia, I thought with vexation, had acted no differently from the most improvident of persons.

'You ought to come to the opera more often,' the Attavanti woman said as soon as we had taken our seats in the box. 'At least when Floria Tosca is singing.'

'Floria Tosca?' I repeated, pretending to ransack my memory in search of something to connect with that name.

'Do not say that you don't know her!' she continued, heedless of the stormy overture begun by the orchestra at that moment. 'It would seem that besides neglecting the theatre you are also staying away from receptions; there is not one worthy of the name recently at which Tosca has not featured as an attraction.'

'Really?'

'I myself, you know, have invited her to sing at my house next week, at a little entertainment for very close friends. Of course you too are among those invited, assuming that your well-known misanthropy should allow you to participate.'

'I thank you, I shall do all within my power not to miss it. So you have taken up this singer and become her protectress.'

'She has no need of protectors now. The whole city admires her, she is the idol...'

'Now that I think of it,' I interrupted her, 'I must have met her once, fleetingly. Perhaps at your cousin's house.'

'Many, baron, would envy the coldness with which you speak of her. That woman has the whole of society at her feet, or at least the male half of it.'

'Men,' observed the niece, affecting an impartial judgement, 'seem to have an uncontrollable impulse to throw themselves at the feet of women of a certain sort.'

'Alas, dearest, not at yours. However, her physical appearance is not the only attraction she has; hearing her sing, it must be admitted, is like listening to the choir of angels in paradise.'

I knit my brows. 'Dear friend, I take the liberty of reminding you of the old adage: do not profane, even in jest...'

'Come now, be not so unbending! And before you dispute the accuracy of my comparison, at least wait until the end of the first act. But on the subject of holy things, you must be aware that our family chapel has been desecrated.'

'Indeed, I do. I did not venture to refer to the matter for fear of intruding on your leisure with unpleasant thoughts, but since you yourself have brought it up I must assure you that investigations are already under way and nothing will be overlooked in the search for the culprit.'

'Above all, try to recover the painting. It may not be a masterpiece, yet I have seen worse, and in any case to commission another would be too costly. Do you have any idea, dear baron, how much painters expect to be paid these days?'

I was glad that the raising of the curtain cut short that conversation. I was disconcerted to notice that the scenery for the first act was identical to that for the third; obviously painters these days expect to be paid too much even for backdrops. Two minor soloists, a bass and a tenor, took up the centre of the stage as their lines went back and forth in a long-winded recitative. Tosca was saving her entrance for later.

'Tell me, marchesa, that singer of whom you were speaking. . .'

'She will come on stage soon. I see you are impatient; I must have aroused your curiosity.'

'Curiosity is an indispensable component of my profession.'

We were interrupted by applause so uproarious that it drowned out the orchestra. I turned towards

the stage and I saw Floria Tosca stepping slowly and
solemnly into the spotlight. She wore the gold tunic,
and her raven-black mane fell on to her shoulders.

'There she is,' the marchesa informed me.
'Delightful, is she not?'

'Most delightful, in her way,' the niece cut in, 'but
perhaps a trifle too dark. The hair, especially. . .'

'Yes, I think so too,' I agreed, winning an almost
affectionate look from the niece. I fancy she would
have gone so far as to smile at me were such a thing
not manifestly at odds with her habitual demeanour.

'Black-eyed and black-haired and so pale of com-
plexion. There is something dissonant in her,
something faintly monstrous.'

'Dear signorina, you have taken the words out of
my mouth.'

All the while I did not take my eyes off Floria
Tosca, who, now in the spotlight, held out her arms
in a dramatic gesture.

'Marchesa, are you sure that this is the first act?'

'What a thing to ask! We have just arrived!'

I was not listening to her. On Tosca's left wrist I
thought I discerned a glitter of gold, but for just a
moment; almost at once she lowered her arms and
I could no longer see anything.

'Do you feel unwell?' the Attavanti woman asked
solicitously.

'I am very well, thank you. Only, of late my
eyesight has grown somewhat weaker, and following
the performance from this distance tires me
overmuch.'

'Niece dear, you really ought to let the baron have
your opera glasses.'

She obeyed, albeit with bad grace, but once I had procured the precious instrument I hesitated to raise it to my eyes. In reality my eyesight was not at all weakened, and with the help of the opera glasses I would be able to inspect Tosca's figure down to the very last details. I would be able to ascertain without a shadow of a doubt whether the glitter on her wrist was really what I supposed it to be or if instead I was deceiving myself. I myself did not know what at that moment I hoped for and what I feared.

The two ladies in the box were giving me perplexed looks and I realised that, having borrowed the opera glasses, I would need to use them. So I brought them to my eyes and set about observing now one, now another corner of the stage, carefully avoiding its centre. After all, no one was compelling me to rest my eyes on Tosca, I was free for the entire duration of the act to contemplate the Corinthian temple or the white moon painted on the backdrop. But very soon the uncertainty in which I deliberately kept myself by adopting that procedure came to seem intolerable, more intolerable than any denial or confirmation which reality could give to my conjectures. My mind made up, I therefore pointed the opera glasses at the centre of the stage and focused them. The golden glitter on Tosca's wrist now flagrantly revealed itself to be that of a bracelet, and more precisely that of a broad smooth circlet, resembling, were it not for its material, one of those rings fixed to the walls of Paradise.

Tosca was singing, the orchestra was no doubt playing, and perhaps the Attavanti woman and her niece were turning towards me to comment on the performance, but I heard nothing. Only after some minutes did I rouse myself and hand back the opera glasses.

'Thank you, signorina,' I said, amazed to discover that I still had control of my voice. 'And my thanks to you, marchesa, for your hospitality. I am compelled to take my leave now; you understand, commitments that cannot be broken. . .'

'You cannot wish to leave so soon.'

'I am sorry, but I must run.'

And I did indeed run, in the most literal sense of the word, even forgetting to make my way to the cloakroom, not stopping until I was outside the theatre.

I took one of the carriages in the square.

'Where to, sir?' asked the coachman.

'Home, and hurry.'

'Yes, sir, but where do you live?'

I told him and he gave me another, more attentive look. 'Forgive me, signor baron, I did not recognise you.' Swiftly he mounted on to the box and whipped the horses on.

I caught sight of myself in the glass of a window. It was not surprising that the man had not recognised me; above the deep shadows from the sleepless nights my gaze had lost its usual firmness, not being seated in the irises but floating on them like a ship riding at anchor. This woman, I thought, can turn everything into a weapon, even happiness.

XI

IT MUST HAVE BEEN almost one; a while before I had heard midnight strike and I had listened out, striving absurdly to distinguish among the different peals that broke into the silence of the night the particular chime of the bells in that church. They had, I was sure, their own voice like no other, one unknown to me for all that, but I would of course have been able to recognise it had I only managed to discern it.

Naturally nothing of the kind came about. When the final tolling of the final bell was over, my state of mind one of vague disappointment, I busied myself once more with the correspondence which had been my occupation since the afternoon. As usual, I rejected the petitions with polite firmness, but at certain moments I was assailed by an inexplicable compassion, by a sense of a sharing in misfortune. Those unhappy beings too were struggling in vain inside the net which gradually tightened around them, imprisoning them ever more securely, and as their confused appeals to my clemency were doomed to go unheard, so I turned in search of succour and support to a God who seemed not to listen. My heavenly patron had obviously turned His back on me, abandoning me defenceless to the onslaughts of another power, a power to which for brevity's sake in my thoughts I gave the name of Maria Triumphant, and from which not even a triply-bolted lock was enough to protect me.

The city was silent, the servants had withdrawn to their quarters, even the moon had now gone down, and in that total solitude, or rather, alone in the company of the demon who had taken possession of me, I composed letters of refusal which were unwontedly concise and bereft, I myself realised, of any force of persuasion. Only in signing the death sentences did I find some mild comfort; Baron Scarpia, no longer master of his own life, still however had mastery of the lives of others.

I was just savouring that slim consolation when a noise startled me. This was a series of decisive blows so distinctly audible that at first I believed them to be very close, even coming from inside the building. But at that hour everyone in the building was asleep, which meant that these blows must be coming from outside. I looked out of the window and saw a figure wrapped in a black cloak banging the heavy knocker on the street door.

I moved away from the window at once. She cannot be sure of finding me here, I thought; I need only not open the door, stick firmly to my purpose, and she will soon go away. Meanwhile, however, the blows continued, with increasing violence so that I feared they would awake not only the porter, but the whole neighbourhood. Before long lights would go on in the houses across the way and men and women in their night-shirts would lean out through the windows to see what was happening, and they would discover Floria Tosca, the famous singer, knocking on Baron Scarpia's door in the depths of the night. In dismay, I seized hold of a candlestick and rushed down the stairs. Immediately on opening the door I took Tosca's arm and pulled her into the entrance hall.

'Are you mad? Did you want the whole city to hear you?'

'I wanted you to hear me,' she answered icily, wrapping herself more tightly in the long cloak. 'Had you opened the door at once. . .'

'So you believe that I should remain here night and day at your disposal, ready to receive you at any time? At this hour respectable people are usually asleep.'

She surveyed me from top to toe. 'In a frock coat?'

'My habits of dress are no concern of yours. You will leave by the back door and perhaps avoid notice.'

'You will allow me at least to explain the reason for my visit.'

'Speak, but I ask you to be brief.'

She looked around the inhospitable darkness of the entrance hall. 'You would not wish to receive me here.'

'I should not wish to receive you at all, signorina, but if you insist. . . Come, I shall show you the way.'

I went back up the stairs with Tosca behind me. We did not exchange a single word until we were in the study, where she slumped on to a sofa as if overcome by great tiredness. She was somewhat out of breath and her expression was halfway between rage and bewilderment.

'The painting,' she said without preliminaries. 'Has disappeared.'

'To which painting are you referring?'

'To *Maria Triumphant*, painted by Mario Cavaradossi. This evening, before the performance, I went to church to collect myself in prayer. When I entered the chapel I saw that the wall above the altar was bare.'

I sat down beside her. 'And you needed so urgently to tell me this? Besides, signorina, you arrive late with your news; I have been aware of the theft for some days now and only yesterday I discussed it with the marchesa Attavanti.'

'You should have discussed it with me.'

'With you? I was unaware that this painting belonged to you.'

She rested a hand on the arm of the sofa, revealing the wrist clasped with the golden circle. As soon as she realised this she withdrew it and concealed it under her cloak again. 'It does not belong to me, that is true, according to the laws of property. But according to those of feeling. . .'

I shrugged. 'The defence of such laws, dear signorina, does not come under my responsibilities.'

'It was I, you know, who was the model for the painting.'

'Indeed?' I said with a show of indifference.

'And to it are linked so many cherished memories.'

I rose. 'All this is very interesting, but if you have nothing else to tell me. . .'

'You, perhaps, should tell me something. I presume that you are carrying out enquiries.'

'I do not see how the matter should concern you. Admittedly, you posed for the painting, yet your reaction seems to me excessive; they stole a canvas after all, they did not abduct you.'

'But in some sense, baron, those who took possession of the canvas have also taken possession of me. This person commands total power over my likeness.'

'You have a morbid sensibility, dear Tosca. And the fact that you identify yourself to such an extent with the image of the Holy Virgin is certainly no testimony in favour of your modesty. *Benedicta in mulieribus*, is that not true? Do you believe this of yourself?'

'I do not understand you, signore.'

'Oh no, you understand me very well. Whoever took away the painting has undoubtedly committed a grave sin, but at least he should be congratulated for having managed to chastise your pride.'

'If that were so, he would succeed where you have failed.'

I smiled. 'Are you sure of that? There are things, my dear, which you still do not know.'

'For example?'

I was in a quandary. I realised I was about to commit an indiscretion, but on the other hand this woman had challenged me openly. At that moment I felt I was ready to place myself altogether in her hands, if only to show her that she was in mine.

'I have you in my grip, signorina, more surely than you realise.'

'You are raving, baron.'

'If you will have the goodness to follow me, before long my point of view will become clearer to you.'

'Follow you? Where to?'

'To Paradise.'

She stared at me with a troubled look. When she got up I thought she meant to leave; instead, she stood motionless, waiting, while the anxiety on her face gradually gave way to an expression of solemn bravery.

'Assuming, of course, that you are not afraid.'

'Lead on,' she answered in a sure voice.

The stone staircase which leads to Paradise is narrow and steep, and I held the candle high so as to light the way for Tosca. She ascended with a step so light as to oblige me every now and then to turn around and assure myself of her presence, and each time she would counter my enquiring look with an extraordinarily determined one, as if to exhort me to proceed. She would not go back now; she would follow me at all costs over that threshold. As I unlocked the door she held the candlestick, bringing it as close to me as possible to make my task easier, and between us was a silence which neither dared to break.

After closing the door behind her I took the candle from her and went to light the torches. We were bathed in a dim reddish glow. Tosca stood before the great brazier, where embers still burned.

'It is used to make the irons red hot,' I said going over to her.

'I had guessed so.'

She looked around and her attention came to rest upon the rack. 'And what is this for?'

I explained, at first with some reticence, then, since she listened without batting an eyelid, in detail, illustrating its workings for her step by step. She listened to me with serene concentration, while the glimmer of the torchlight was reflected on her face, changing its pallor into an unnatural brightness.

Encouraged, I also showed her the wheel and then the so-called throne, a somewhat sophisticated instrument which I use solely to reduce the most recalcitrant victims to reason; at the mere sight of it Count Palmieri had fainted. Tosca inspected it without a tremor, and kept on asking me for clarification. Her questions were probing and pertinent, her quickness to understand the answers worthy of an initiate. Without a doubt she made up for her lack of experience with an innate disposition for the subject. At every moment her look insisted that if I had meant to frighten her I might as well give up, but at the same time it seemed to express a more complex feeling which I could not manage to decipher.

Leading her round in this slow exploration, I myself observed the room with different eyes, and was fascinated by it almost as if like her I had entered for the first time. It was no longer the prosaically domestic place in which I was used to expedite my duties, but a magic world where everything alluded to secret exchanges between life and death, between suffering and bliss. I suddenly recalled a theory according to which the same stimulus which arouses pleasure when it does not surpass a given intensity, beyond it reaches pain, and I wondered whether over that threshold there might not be another, and whether for whoever dared to cross it there might not be reserved, in pain itself, an infinite pleasure.

'Yes,' I said out loud, 'so long as the sensation shifts from minus to plus again . . .'

'What?'

'Nothing, I was considering some theoretical possibilities. Perhaps I should add a new chapter to my treatise on the aesthetic of torture.'

'Will you let me read it?'

'Why should I?'

'Since you thought of it just now it must mean that I was the one to inspire it.'

I smiled, while in my heart I strove to deny all validity to that hypothesis. 'It would seem, dear Tosca, that you are an excellent inspiration: to painters. . .'

'And to torturers.'

'I shall therefore choose you as my muse, if it pleases you, and I shall dedicate all my works to you from now on.'

I could not help but admire her; in that place of tears she was able to maintain the brilliant and aloof demeanour which she might have assumed in a drawing room conversing on topics without importance. Yet what happened in here was in no way without importance to her; I guessed this from the way in which she pulled her cloak close around her as if in that black cloth she sought refuge from what surrounded her. And her imperturbability was too flagrant, it betrayed an anxiety to hide, to dissemble.

'So, dear Tosca, what do you think?'

'About what, baron?'

I pointed to the instruments of Paradise, bringing them all together with a broad, impartial gesture; thus a father would show all his beloved children together to a visitor, refusing to establish any order of preference between them.

'To be honest, I expected worse,' she answered in the tone of a disappointed connoisseur.

'Worse? But did you look well?'

'You see, I had imagined this place ... not very often, of course, but a couple of times I had indeed imagined it. . .'

'And so?'

'And so, the reality does not match the imagination. If you wished to frighten me, dear Scarpia, you should not have brought me here.'

'Many, signorina, are frightened by it,' I retorted coldly. 'Perhaps their imagination is not so lively as yours.'

'Perhaps.' She drew her hand over a row of whips which hung from a wall. 'But you see, here everything remains ... on this side of a certain threshold.'

I was disconcerted by the diabolical skill which this woman succeeded in entering into my thoughts. Or perhaps it was she herself who inspired them in me, like some malign muse. It became increasingly clear to me that in this place some will was bent with total determination towards a purpose, but I still was unable to grasp the nature of this purpose, and I did not even know whose will this was, whether mine, Tosca's, or some other made up of both and at the same time transcending them. It was undoubtedly this will which placed the reference to the threshold on Tosca's lips, and which made me respond as I did.

'Yet, a threshold which could be crossed.'

'And how?'

'I have not yet shown you everything. Indeed, I have not shown you the most important thing.'

'The prototype for a new rack? A special wheel invented by you?'

'Do you remember what I told you in the study? You are already over the threshold, even if you do not realise it.'

I took her arm and led her to a niche closed with heavy double doors of iron.

'Be patient, I must find the key... Here it is... The light is dim, I admit, but there is enough for you to be able to recognise...'

I put the key in the lock, turned it three times and opened the doors wide. The red glow of the torches revealed the gold tunic of Maria Triumphant, the white white face, the hand pressed upon the serpent's head, while the mane of hair was lost in the darkness.

I turned towards Tosca. She was motionless, her eyes fixed on the painting; only her fingers moved, convulsively gripping the edge of her cloak.

'Really, Floria, did you not know?'

I said it sweetly, shyly; I was afraid I had gone too far in showing her the painting, her rigid bearing seemed to express deep indignation. Before long, I thought, she would turn and leave the room.

Instead she remained rapt before the painting, and after a while turned her eyes on me. Unclasping her fingers, she allowed the cloak to fall to the floor. She was wearing the thin gold tunic, her stage costume for *The Triumph of Virtue*.

In her eyes I read surrender, but not to me; she was yielding rather to that will to which I myself had bent, to which I had been subject ever since I had entered Paradise with Tosca, or maybe before, maybe since the day when, hidden in the darkness of the nave, I had watched her at prayer. As if performing an action prescribed for all time, I went up to her and loosened the ribbon which held back her hair. With the same almost liturgical resolve she answered my gesture by undoing her belt. The gold tunic slid to the ground and left her body totally naked but for her feet which still had the golden straps of the sandals wound about them.

Our eyes were alert, our movements controlled. We both felt that whatever was now happening was removed from the arbitrary, from freedom, even from desire. All of this had been left behind, on the other side of the threshold; now we found ourselves in a world where nothing could be changed, in a realm of limpid necessity of whose laws we had suddenly become the guardians.

He who before crossing the threshold had been Baron Scarpia took the hand of she who had been Floria Tosca and led her to a wall from which two rings protruded. She held out her arms to put her wrists through them. He locked the rings, making sure he had tightened them enough, then went over to a cabinet from which he drew a thin chain. He went back to her and knelt before her. He undid one of the sandals and took it off, then undid the other which she slipped off with a push from her naked foot. He put the chain around one ankle. At that moment the eyes of both turned to the great painting hung in the niche, then they moved away from it and met. He abased himself again. She slowly lifted the foot that was free and pressed it down upon his head, firmly. At last the pressure eased, but before getting up he remained on his knees for a few moments, absorbed in his own sensations. It was at that point in the ritual that there was revealed to him the meaning of the word 'fulfilment'.

✜ XII ✜

'FULFILMENT' in Latin is *explectio*, from *expleo*, to fill up. It is a brimming or a brimming over, whereby the full measure of the self's being is reached; this is why 'fulfilment' is also *perfectio*, perfection, which implies an ending reached. One is perfected, and one dies, or else time keeps on idling, while the mind remains fixed upon the moment when fulfilment occurred as at some extreme limit beyond which there is nothing more.

From the aesthetic point of view this prolongation is redundant; much more beautiful is the way in which one of the humblest of creatures, the tick, accomplishes its destiny. It spends its whole life sitting on a branch waiting to discover the warmth of some animal's body, then it throws itself upon this, consumes its only meal of blood and dies sated, probably happy. In such a simple scheme as this there is a touching rigour, an exemplary classicism. I might even envy it were I not held back by the thought that a tick could never have known Floria Tosca. And since we go through life seeking, and

swinging continually between opposing and contra-
dictory principles, it is all the sweeter for us to
achieve a sudden glimpse of the goal for which we
were ever destined, the hidden meaning to which our
tangled instincts inclined across countless vicious
circles; while the tick, poor thing, knows right from
the start what it wants and pursues it with implacable directness; for the tick there is neither struggle
nor conquest, nor self-mastery. The fact is that being
a tick plainly does not amount to much, but
becoming one represents the supreme bliss.

When we meet again I shall tell Tosca about this
small parasite, and about *perfectio* and its ambiguous
etymology. No doubt she knows all this, but she
lacks a rational consciousness of it, a lucid expo-
sition.

(N.B. In the moment of greatest pleasure, as in
that of greatest pain, men and women very often
close their eyes. Work through the implications of
this fact systematically.)

The negators of the negative should be honest
enough to admit that without it the positive would
be reduced to a very paltry thing. Without it, for
example, Tosca's gaze would in fact be inconceivable.
There is therefore necessarily a negative aspect in
the idea of perfection, even in its theological appli-
cation. It seems to me increasingly difficult
otherwise to understand the divine essence than as
an abyss where good lives alongside evil, alongside
sin, and where both are equally legitimated. Until
yesterday, I suspected nothing of this; I believed I

served the Whole by serving one part. It is as if Its face, veiled before, were now all at once uncovered for me in Its entirety.

Or else I have always known it, and what is happening to me is only *perfectio*, the fulfilment of what I confusedly foresaw. My half-awareness was joined to Tosca's half-awareness to make up a total awareness, full to the brim, almost brimming over in its excess lucidity. For I now see everything clearly, and she too, I am sure, sees everything clearly.

We know we must end, but for now it will still be allowed us to play with annihilation, each to push forward and hold back the other, in a mysterious balance, on the borderline.

My dear,
I order you to come to me on the stroke of midnight. At that hour the servants will have retired, so that we run no risks. And be mindful not to come battering on the main door; I shall leave the back door ajar for you so that you can enter without being observed by the neighbours. No one must meddle in our affairs, so that if we preserve the integrity of our reputation by continuing to show a proud face to all, we will be able to keep on enjoying the pleasure of stripping ourselves bare of all that for one another, of each in turn sacrificing our pride. If you were not Floria Tosca it would not be so miraculous to see you cease to be her, therefore take good care of your prideful mask, as I intend to do with that of Baron Scarpia.

I order you moreover to wear the gold tunic. I

know that there is no need to say so, certain things go without saying, but I am punctilious by nature, some think even pedantic. Besides, you are the last person in the world to have any grounds for complaint about this (at least, last night you seemed to find my severity in no way displeasing), and therefore I permit myself to stipulate that the sandals too must be the same ones. And do not dare appear before me without the gold bracelet.

Enough, for now I have no more orders for you. I shall receive you at midnight precisely; in the meantime, Baron Scarpia has the honour of paying his most devoted respects to Floria Tosca.

The hours go by with exasperating slowness. Often, my men slip the usual messages under the door, messages in which I cannot manage to take the slightest interest. Arousing great astonishment, I have halted the interrogations until further notice and I have forbidden anyone to open the door of Paradise; no one else must set foot there again, such desecration would be intolerable to me, but of course I cannot cite this reason, which means I must pretend to be indisposed. In any case such a thing could well be true, the excitement overwhelming me could very well be taken for a malaise, and perhaps it really is so. This morning I looked in the mirror and had trouble recognising myself, the customary composure having deserted my face, giving way to the expression of a drunken man. Who knows how Tosca looks now, in the light of day; I would have liked to be there when she awoke, to see her feature transfigured as she regained consciousness and brought to mind the hours spent with me. Certainly at that moment she must have borne an extraordinary resemblance to Maria Triumphant.

They tell me, by the way, that Cavaradossi has finally been captured. The news is altogether a matter of indifference to me, and I imagine it is for her too by now. They wanted to bring him here, but fortunately I managed to prevent it; I should not have known what to do with him, where to put him. So he will be imprisoned in an ordinary jail and someone else will see to his interrogation. It would at this point be childish to wish for revenge, absurd to be jealous; he has never known the woman who was with me in Paradise, nor has he even an inkling of her existence. Doubtless he had with her only mediocre relations, the stuff of sugary caresses and insipid affections. Only in painting the picture does he seem to have guessed at something different, hinting with the paintbrush at a truth his mind could not grasp. How narrow and tiresome his ideals now appear to me, how blind before the austere majesty of what overpowers us! Until yesterday, some echo of all this was still on Tosca's lips. The God of goodness, the God of mercy... In the name of Heaven, why be limited to so one-sided a vision? The God of love? Yes, perhaps this says everything.

My dearest,
Yesterday I awaited you in vain. And no word from you all day, not even two lines of explanation. Do you perhaps believe that between us there is nothing more to add? I myself, I must confess,

have suspected this at times; there is little left for anyone who has driven himself as far as we two drove ourselves, perhaps one thing only. But if it is not given to us to act we can at least remember together, or rather, each thing we do would be from now on a remembering, each present the repetition of that past. I do not know whether you have ever felt what deep peace, what sublime assurance is released by the idea of repetition; in it perhaps is locked the only form of innocence possible upon this earth.

So, with you, I would gladly repeat, just as my whole life before has been nothing but an anticipation, a step-by-step ascent to the dizzy heights of those hours. You too, I am sure, regard your past in the same way, for you too that night must have marked a caesura, the start of a new era, and perhaps you are so overpowered by those events that you can scarcely find the strength to write me a note. Yes, this is without a doubt the most likely interpretation of your silence, but, forgive me for saying so, I should prefer to see you express this state of mind in a less indirect manner.

And after all it is untrue that there is nothing to be added; I must tell you of the tick, a topic of enormous interest, and I also planned to illustrate for you the etymology of the term 'fulfilment', even although your demeanour leads me to maintain that you have already divined it. Come in any case tonight at twelve precisely. Remember that you owe me obedience, and be sure not to be late; as you know my punishments can be terrible.

*

The victim of genius, she who takes the whole world into herself. The only one with whom the torturer can manage to identify. Deepen this intuition, perhaps citing some examples. Problem: what would become of the torturer, were such a victim to be taken away from him?

XIII

LAST NIGHT TOO my waiting was in vain; I stayed up until sunrise and listened out in the hope of hearing the creak of the little door at the back. I waited stubbornly, obdurately, even although by the time midnight was just past my thought was not 'She is late', but rather 'She will not come'. It was for certain not indifference that kept her away; it might have been fear, the sense of having gone too far, which was also mingled, in a counterpoint both distressing and exciting, with my anxiety to see her again. In truth there is something terrible in the idea of seeing again the person with whom one has crossed the threshold, the person who has wrenched us away from ourselves to deliver us into the hands of a power which cannot be mastered; and yet, I mused, how can such a meeting be rejected when around it there now gravitated the whole of exist-ence, not only mine but, I was quite convinced of it, Tosca's too? It did not seem to me that ticks, once they had perceived the smell of an animal, could behave as if nothing had happened and stay unperturbed on the branch. No, one had to plunge in, like it or not, and sooner or later she would realise this. For now however it had become my lot to endure this cruel wavering of hers, who could say for how much longer.

It was already morning and I was just about to doze off on a sofa when I heard knocking. One of my servants, a somewhat doltish young man, half-opened the double doors and stood timidly in the doorway.

I sat up. 'What do you want? Don't you know that it is forbidden to disturb me?'

'Forgive me, signor baron, but someone must still deliver your correspondence.'

'The rule is that it is to be left on the desk when I am not here.'

'Yet, signor baron, lately you are always here.'

This boy's reasoning, I was compelled to acknowledge, was not bereft of logic. 'Well, what are you waiting for? Hand me the mail and go; I wish to be left alone.'

He promptly obeyed, his face showing unmistakable signs of relief as he withdrew.

Besides the usual pleadings and petitions, the morning post brought me a note from the marchesa Attavanti. I opened it absentmindedly, imagining that she was writing for news of the painting.

'Dear Baron,
You have given no reply to the note which I sent you some days ago, neither to accept the invitation nor decline it, therefore I must suppose that you have completely forgotten about my small

entertainment. You high-placed functionaries, one knows, are beset by countless troublesome things, and in several respects you resemble artists in their dreamy disposition. Taking this into consideration, I forgive your unforgivable discourtesy and renew the invitation; if you wish to come I shall expect you this afternoon from five o'clock onwards. Otherwise stay just where you are and accept the most respectful regards of Your. . .'

The invitation had altogether gone out of my mind and, rather more seriously, what the marchesa had told me that evening at the theatre, that Floria Tosca would sing to entertain the distinguished guests, had also gone out of my mind. I would therefore see her again within a few hours, whether she liked it or not.

Immediately I wrote a few lines in answer:

'Dear Marchesa,
Whatever am I thinking of these days? With humility and contrition I offer you my most heartfelt apologies and I thank you for the kindness shown by you towards this reprobate. For me, of course, it will be a pleasure, besides being an honour, to be with you this afternoon at five o'clock precisely.'

I rang the bell, and on the reappearance of the even more intimidated young man I handed him the note for delivery. Now, I thought, it is only a matter of waiting until five.

Since there was nearly half a day to go I tried to

distract my mind with work, on which however I could not manage to concentrate. I opened a book, but having reached the end of the first paragraph I realised that my eyes had scanned the lines without the slightest involvement on the part of my intellect. So I lay down on the couch again, resigned to giving up the whole morning to anticipation.

Has no one ever remarked how much idleness, if excessively prolonged, can be exhausting? I ended those hours spent doing nothing worn out as if from the heaviest exertion. After a frugal meal I had myself shaved and combed, perfumed and dressed, giving up my body to the servants with total inertia. By three I had already had the horses harnessed; at four I was outside the gates of the Attavanti palace.

Even in my daze, I recalled that a gentleman cannot present himself at the house of strangers an hour in advance, and I recalled that I was a gentleman. I would therefore return later; meanwhile, in order to cheat that time which was so reluctant to be cheated I decided to take a walk.

I am almost certain that I did not intend to go there, it was by pure chance that I found myself there, yet when I realised that I was in the alley I looked for Tosca's house and raised my eyes up to the window. The curtains were drawn and I could see nothing, not even the tiniest movement beyond the screen of muslin. She was probably already at the Attavanti palace rehearsing her arias.

My thoughts returned to the evening when through those same windows I had seen her shadow embracing the shadow of Cavaradossi; a few weeks ago according to the standard measurement of time, but in this short period the passage from darkness to light, from blindness to clear-sightedness had taken place, burying all that had occurred before in a distant past which I could scarcely recognise as my own. It seemed to me that an epoch had gone by since the first time I had made my way along the cobblestones of the alley, and the deep transformation, the radical upheaval of my whole being made it inappropriate to attribute the experiences of then and those of now to the same subject.

I went past the church and turned away, stricken with feelings of guilt. And yet, I told myself, there was no guilt in me; Maria Triumphant had called and I had answered, simply, inevitably, in obedience to the law which had been predestined for me. What did it matter if others defined this obedience as transgression, crime or sacrilege, when such definitions are only the fruit of boundless presumption, of erroneous conviction. Certainly, were there some will outside the law, will could break the law; but since the law itself dictates to each his will, the two terms are really synonymous, so it is to be concluded that believing in the possibility of guilt constitutes the most abominable of heresies.

Standing apart, I observed the pious old women come out of mass. Some were bent double as they walked, as if with the years the burden of life had broken their backs; on the faces of others I read the miserly satisfaction of having confessed some paltry peccadillo to the priest and having been absolved of it. They went through the alley in tight groups, while exchanging glances of malign distrust. And yet, I thought, every thing is innocent in this world, every destiny is just, there is no punishment, only the incomprehensible majesty of pain. And at that moment it seemed to me that there is something ghastly locked within the notion of innocence.

As my mind digressed so too with it did my steps, and I had trouble finding the way to the Attavanti palace. I reached it a little late; there were already numerous carriages parked at the front and on both sides of the gates were arrayed footmen in livery.

Since around two hundred people had been invited to the 'little entertainment for very close friends' a patient search was needed before I could locate the marchesa.

'Ah, Baron,' she said as soon as she saw me. 'It is a rare privilege to have you among us.'

'The privilege is mine.'

Almost at once the niece came up to us dressed in a simple, high-necked garment. 'So,' she remarked sourly, 'you too have come to admire Floria Tosca.'

'I have come, signorina, to pay my most devoted respects to you and your aunt, the marchesa. As for the singer, I do not even know if I shall have time to stay and hear her.'

'Ah, but you *must* hear her, without question,' exclaimed the marchesa. 'It would really be a sin. . .'

'A sin from which, I am sure, you would absolve me with your usual magnanimity. It would however be opportune for you to introduce me to this person, to . . . yes, to Floria Tosca, before the performance.'

'Of course. But you will most surely wish to greet His Eminence.'

'Later, if you do not mind.'

'And the princess? She was asking after you a little while ago.'

'Later, dear marchesa. You see, there are grave reasons which make my meeting this person a matter of great urgency.'

'You refer perhaps to the Cavaradossi affair?'

'I, marchesa, have said nothing, my lips are sealed as always, but I certainly cannot prevent you from exercising your feminine intuition.'

'So you have come for professional reasons,' said the niece with visible relief.

'Once again, signorina, I have said nothing.'

'I am so offended, baron,' said the aunt, 'that I have almost decided not to introduce you to the singer.'

'Forgive me, I beg you, and introduce me to her; you will thereby render a most valuable service to justice.'

'So be it, come with me.'

Without dropping her aggrieved manner she led me through the tight groups of guests, stopping from time to time to engage someone in pointless conversation to which I, involved against the grain, would contribute some casual remark. These incessant pauses exasperated me, especially after I had seen Floria sitting in an armchair just a few steps away and yet separated from me by an ocean of pleasantries. I had expected to find her surrounded by admirers, and yet she was alone, seemingly resolved to protect her solitude by maintaining a severe demeanour.

'Please, marchesa, let us go on.'

'There is plenty of time, your zeal is truly excessive. Ah, dear countess, what a magnificent outfit?'

'Do you think so?'

'Indeed I do. Sooner or later I shall be unfaithful to my dressmaker with yours.'

Meanwhile I was observing Tosca's outfit, a sumptuous gown of dark red silk, and I wondered why no one had ever thought of adopting red as the colour of mourning. In her entire appearance, as in her posture, there was however something of the widow, a painful gravity which I was at a loss to explain. I had besides the odd feeling that she was missing something.

'There is His Eminence over there; come and speak to him.'

'Dear friend, I have already explained. . .'

'It is a matter of a few minutes, justice will be none the worse for it. Eminence, this evening we have an unaccustomed guest.'

As I bent to kiss the cardinal's ring, all at once I understood the reason for the impression of incompleteness which Tosca's attire had given me.

'The bracelet!' I exclaimed.

'What are you saying, my son?'

'Forgive me, Your Eminence; before meeting you I was following an inner train of thought, and only now has the solution leapt before my eyes.'

'I understand, my son, and I forgive you, but if you will allow me I should like to give you some advice.'

'I am flattered by such kindness.'

'The great zeal with which you dedicate yourself to your profession is known to everyone, Baron

Scarpia; yet, have you never chanced to wonder that in this too there might lurk some snare of the devil?'

'In my profession, Your Eminence?'

'In your zeal, my beloved son, in the excessive zeal with which you execute it.'

'The marchesa, I believe, is of the same opinion. But I beg to differ. . .'

'It would be well to give to the world what is of the world, and not to remain outside the society of one's peers.'

'You see me here this evening, in the society of my peers.'

'I am glad of it, and I should be even more glad were your appearances not so rare.'

'Alas, Your Eminence, duty. . .'

'My dear son, sometimes external necessities change into inner necessities, habit into vice, and you, allow me to say so, indulge excessively in the vice of solitude.'

I was scarcely able to listen to him, distracted as I was by the image of Tosca's naked arm, her unadorned wrist.

'In this way you will become more vulnerable.'

'Vulnerable?'

'You will succumb more easily to evil, to error; you will diverge from familiar paths, thus with the risk of losing your way.'

'You are right, Your Eminence, I recognise this,' I said in a desperate attempt to be free of him. 'I shall try to correct myself.'

'Well done, correct yourself. And if you should need my counsel again. . .'

'Certainly, Your Eminence. For now, I thank you

for the courtesy and the paternal indulgence you have shown to me.'

'You are welcome, my son.'

At last I moved away, followed by the marchesa, whom I enjoined to take me at once to Tosca. The latter rose, looking very pale, and from her bewildered expression I realised that she was only now aware of me. With an unconscious gesture her hand reached towards the wrist without its bracelet, whereon there still were to be seen two thin red circles.

'Baron Scarpia, allow me to introduce the signorina Floria Tosca, our welcome guest and the main attraction of the evening.'

I took her hand and held it for a few moments in mine before placing the ritual kiss upon it 'Signorina, it is a great honour for me. . .'

'The honour is mine,' she answered with a slight bow.

'I have admired you once before, some time ago, and I hope I will soon be allowed the opportunity to admire you again.'

'But of course, baron,' intervened the marchesa, who, contrary to my hopes, seemed to have no intention of leaving us alone. 'This very evening.'

'This very evening?' I said staring at Tosca. She said not a word in answer.

'I have already told you,' the Attavanti woman went on, 'that the signorina will sing for us.'

'It is true, you did tell me. And were there to be an aria which we especially liked, would the signorina be good enough to repeat it?'

'Repeat it, baron? I really think not, I'm afraid,' she retorted drily.

'What are you saying, my dear?' said the marchesa in amazement. 'Why not?'

'Because this evening, you see, I intend to sing in a way that is perfect, and that which is perfect cannot be repeated.'

'You are wrong,' I objected. 'On the contrary, I maintain that it *must* be repeated.'

She smiled. 'I have heard it said, baron, that you enjoy the study of philosophy.'

'More than that; of late I have been passionately engaged in studying the habits of a small animal about which I shall tell you perhaps, in a different place. But I am compelled to admit that this animal proves to be thoroughly and in every wise in agreement with you.'

'In agreement with her? Of what are you speaking?'

'I presume, marchesa, that the signorina means to argue that whatever is perfect is necessarily unique, and therefore unrepeatable. Or am I mistaken?'

'No, baron, you are not mistaken. I am glad that you have understood the meaning of my words so promptly.'

'And yet, you know, I believe you are wrong. What is more, I believe that you wish to hide from us the real reason for your refusal.'

'The real reason?'

'Fear, signorina.'

Laughing, she turned to the lady of the house. 'What do you say about that, marchesa? Have I ever seemed fearful to you?'

'No, my dear, not even when you sang in the presence of the Holy Father. There must be some other reason.'

'The most straightforward one: repetitions are tedious.' She turned towards me, her eyes fixed upon me. 'Sometimes, Baron Scarpia, fatally tedious. Try to understand.'

'I understand you, and very well too. But what if we were disposed to die?'

The Attavanti woman cast increasingly perplexed glances at the one and then the other of us. 'And why ever, dear friend, should we be disposed towards such a thing?'

'You are right, signora. Why ever should you? Best to leave everything as it is. I have planned a quite specific programme and I mean to keep to it, assuming that you will allow me.'

'A programme from which repetitions are excluded?' I asked.

'Precisely. Now, if you will excuse me, I think it is time to make my final preparations with the orchestra.'

'Well,' said the marchesa, as soon as Tosca was out of earshot, 'you cannot make so bold as to claim that this silly conversation has been of any help to your investigations.'

'Of enormous help, my dear. Or if you prefer, fatally helpful.'

✤ XIV ✤

YES, TOSCA, I insist on an encore. Or did you imagine
that I would be frightened? Did you imagine, by
singing that aria from the third act in such vengeful
accents, with such cold ferocity, that you would
convince me? 'To plunge into the villain's blood',
well I shall not argue, let it be as you wish; but
revenge for what, in the name of Heaven, and villain
for what sin? You know me to be innocent, dear
Floria, and it is perhaps just this that you cannot
bear. But set aside for once and for all the feeble
wisdom of the two librettists, with their crude
notion of justice, and bring to mind the different
wisdom and the different justice we each learned
from the other on that night.

I do not say this, let it be quite plain, to disarm
you, but if you choose to raise your hand I want at
least for that to happen for true reasons and in utter
knowledge. And I want you to have no illusions
about being able to survive me, as I have had none
of being able to survive that night for long.

For the rest, clearly your every wish will be willingly granted. Clemency for Cavaradossi? So be it, but you must allow me a little ruse, without which I should give the lie to the cruel mask of Baron Scarpia. So it will fall to me to ask you to reward my mercy, and you perhaps will satisfy me; but I am certain that whatever then takes place will not belong to that tired script, that laughable pantomime of noble sentiments, outraged virtues and just vendettas. It will be inscribed rather as a conclusive epiphany of the ritual whose first lines we recited together.

The events of the last weeks offer changed meaning to my changed eyes, and if earlier I spoke of a poison which would have been transmitted to me in church, when I placed my hand on yours, it now seems equally right to define it as a balm, a health-giving essence; I have spoken of an ocean which heaved beneath my feet, but perhaps I already felt the temptation to plunge in, to lose myself within that yielding formlessness.

The view of scholars that nature abhors a void is a strange one. It seems to me on the contrary that the void exerts a powerful attraction over all kinds of creatures; it is proved by the very existence of vertigo, which is simply a mixture of horror and the wish to jump, and therefore it would be inconceivable did there not live in each of us a nostalgia for the abyss. Thus I, ever more seduced, kept on building barriers and parapets in a pathetic attempt to defeat that inner enemy, and only now do I realise how futile it was. Before your whims and threats I am utterly defenceless; not to see you would be as impossible for me as to dispel the force of gravity.

Sometimes I stop writing and lift my eyes to the window. I have opened the curtains, so that nothing bars my sight of the moon; it is white, milky and extraordinarily like the one painted on the backdrop in the third act of *The Triumph of Virtue*, and looks similarly shorn of splendour, a simple circle with wavering outlines traced on the darkness of the sky by a hurried hand. It seems easy tonight to draw the curtain aside and look out, to contemplate the real moon, the real sky and the whole unfathomable landscape of eternity; at such a thought I am stricken again by vertigo, and perhaps my stubborn writing and reasoning is a way of resisting it, of giving form to the desire which impels me more and more towards the formless. In well-ordered sentences, I try to express my foreboding of a world alien to any syntax.

You too strive to oppose vertigo and your intended vendetta forms a part of this striving. You are obviously a prey to the mirage of action as I am to that of thought, you imagine that with an act of violence you can escape a destiny which already is fulfilled. I myself, however, was hesitant to write to you; after our conversation at the Attavanti palace, seeing you again seemed too great a risk and I might have renounced it were it still in my power to choose. On re-entering my study, for some time I even felt a deceptive sense of security, believing that no danger could reach me in this refuge. But danger, Floria, lurks within our hearts, it is another name for that vertigo, for that nostalgia; it lurks within us from the time that together we entered Paradise and together crossed a threshold from which there is no return. Since then I can find neither shelter nor foothold in what surrounds me; not even solitude can cast out your presence.

Sometimes I wonder if I might not have avoided all this, and the happenings which have led me to this point appear as a series of crossroads at each one of which I have resolutely taken the wrong path. Yet each alternative would have meant renunciation of which I cannot bear even to think, an act of barricading myself inside the narrow limits of my own existence. I cannot in truth regret having broken through those limits; too many things would otherwise have stayed unknown to me, precious things, over which it seems petty to me to haggle. No price is too high for the truth, even though I convince myself more and more that salvation lies in error, that the labyrinth of life is more easily travelled with clouded eyes. Seeing means seeing the abyss, from which it then becomes no longer possible to look away; knowing means knowing oneself delivered to annihilation, and outside this no true learning exists.

I could define my pervasive state of mind as resignation, yet this term would do no justice to my intensity of feeling. At the thought of seeing you again I feel a violent disturbance, which can only partly be related to the fear of what perhaps awaits me. Above all, Floria, *I desire* to see you again, I desire it with such force as to regard everything else as secondary, because our meeting will be the supreme moment and it would be absurd to ask ourselves what could come after it. At that moment we shall achieve immortality, and perhaps this requires the secret complicity of death; there are in our lives events which demand the duration of eternity and wrench us with violence away from the dull flow of time, events beside which a physical death is only redundancy, the didactic pedantry of a naive playscript. And should Baron Scarpia let himself be scared by such a commonplace expedient? After having fearlessly overcome the first and second threshold, should he now retreat before the possibility of that rudimentary addition? On the contrary; whatever should happen, I have no doubt that I shall be able to display the greater courage, also because the comforting and glorious thought of Paradise will succour me.

Should we give a name to the divinity worshipped by both of us? I have thought it over well and I have decide to call it love. According to one ancient teaching, love, together with hate, governs the succession of cosmic cycles, but of the two which do you believe is the destructive force, the one which impels individuals to merge together, to erase themselves blissfully, erase themselves in a blurred whole? The world, my dear, exists only as a negation of this love, as its limitation by an opposing power, and only thus do Floria Tosca and Baron Scarpia exist, half measures, the terms of an unsatisfying compromise. We however have left any compromise behind us; by now we are hardly capable of speaking the language of other men, of thoughtlessly employing its euphemisms, of respecting its guile. I realised this today, at the house of the marchesa, when we faced one another like two people newly awakened in a company of sleepwalkers, and I realised what a surprise such an awakening must have been for you, accustomed to understanding the word 'love' in the banal and reassuring sense accepted by Cavaradossi and his like. This is why it does not amaze me that it should be so hard for you to express yourself lucidly in our new language, and I readily forgive you your stammerings and awkwardness and hesitations. I forgive them, it goes without saying, so long as you make every effort to triumph over them for once and all.

Yes, Tosca Triumphant; I give you leave to fulfil this metamorphosis to the very end. Lift the hem of your tunic, raise your foot to crush my head, but stop deluding yourself that these actions belong to you, when you yourself by now no longer belong to you. Do not misunderstand me, I do not presume to make you mine, as lovers sometimes say of one another in their blind language. We, Floria, are not blind, and perhaps we are not lovers either, but rather ministers of love; so render to this power the homage that is due to it.

XV

AS EVENING APPROACHED I went up to Paradise to assure myself that everything was in order. The brazier had gone out. On the wheel, on the rack and on the other instruments a layer of dust was accumulating, whips and lashes hung wanly from the walls. Amid that desolation I found only one sign of life, a long lock of black hair caught in one of the rings; I removed it delicately, promising myself to keep it.

I looked questioningly at Maria Triumphant, almost expecting a response from her, and her expression seemed to me to alter between unfailing severity and infinite pity. *Benedicta tu in mulieribus*, I said aloud, immediately smiling at myself because I found myself absorbed in praying to the portrait of Tosca, and because this gesture, which once I had deemed blasphemous, now seemed to me perfectly natural. I would have knelt in front of the canvas had I had reason to hope that the pleas raised up to the image would have been heard and granted by the flesh and blood woman.

On leaving, however, I left the torches lit and I did not shut the painting up behind the double doors again; everything must be ready to receive Tosca. Perhaps these preparations will truly have the power to compel her to obey me and keep the appointment, as magic words and rituals compel spirits to appear.

When I returned to the study I found a safe place for the lock of hair between the pages of one of my favourite books, and as I closed it I wondered whether I would ever chance to turn its pages again. I asked myself this, I feel I can say it in all conscience, without the least trace of sentimentality or self-pity, but rather in a state of mind of detached curiosity. Then I put the book back on the shelf, sat down at the desk and began to write these notes.

The moon has disappeared from the horizon, yet its light continues to brighten the vault of the sky which appears singularly low and oppressive. A little while ago, in the slumbering city, I heard close on a hundred bells chime out two o'clock in deep harmony. Everything seems drenched in an atmosphere of suspense, as if taking part in my anticipation.

In the middle of the desk, plainly visible and duly signed, is the order for Cavaradossi's release; the execution order, intended to be read by my men, is placed instead in a corner along with the rest. In this way I will at any rate be certain that the sinister fame of Baron Scarpia will long outlive me, perhaps for ever, and yet tonight this certainty is almost a matter of indifference to me. I draw greater consolation from watching the clouds, their slow migrations, the compliance with which they give themselves up to everything which waylays their form. There is really something calming in the spectacle of those fluid, scantly shaped existences, which are continuously on the point of melting back into nothingness.

But perhaps the moment has come. I fancy I hear the faint creak of the back door. I fancy I hear Tosca's footsteps on the stairs. I am ready to receive her, all uncertainty is now far, far away. Allow him the time still to write these words, then Baron Scarpia will lay down his pen, close his notebook and go to meet what awaits him.